The Pastor's Wife

By Y A Leone

---

1.   http://www.unsplash.com

Dedication

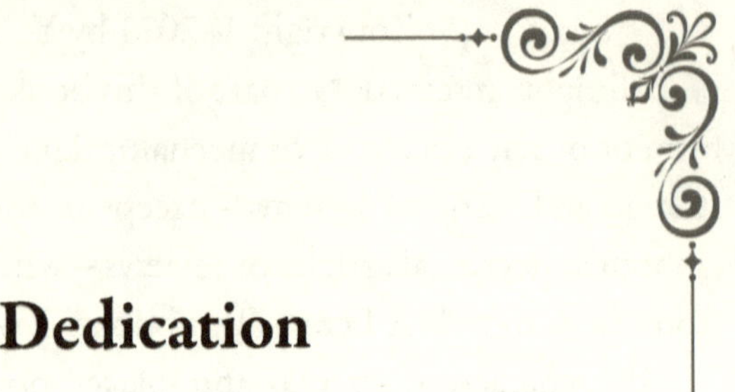

To my loved ones who continue supporting my dream. Thank you so much. To God the Father and the very source of my life and being.

Prologue

BETH STARED IN DISBELIEF as Mrs. Williams spelt out the judgment for her. She had pulled down her reading glasses and was peering above them, glaring disapprovingly at the tiny girl clutching on the armrest of a chair as she pronounced, "We have come to the conclusion that Beth should terminate her pregnancy or be excommunicated from the church. We can't have her bad mouthing the pastor's son can we?" The decision had been made after a long session of debating and hearing both sides to the story from the couple in question. Jeffrey her partner in crime was still adamant in that he didn't date her and to top it all up, he claimed Beth was obsessed with him. With her pert nose held high at such a claim, she also remained resolute in her statement that he was being cowardly and they had indeed been involved.

The women in the board rather thought the whole idea preposterous for the pastor's son to date the maid's daughter and hence kept on goading Beth to admit to what they deemed the truth. Finally the decision was reached and all eyes were focused on the girl as the boy had already left for his home. *This is not fair,* Beth thought. Her eyes pleaded for someone to rescue her from the wretched women. Her mother was staring at the ceiling, oblivious to the events taking place as Beth clutched at her heart, feeling the injustice pressing heavily on it.

Walls were closing in on her from both ends, taking away her very breath as she panted for more of the air and not the fear she felt which was about to overwhelm her as the notable women in church would rather defend the culprit while the victim suffered. It had all been a lie, she thought. Gone was the Jeffrey she knew who followed her like a love sick puppy. In his place stood a smartly dressed, dark haired, cold blooded young man, with a slight curl on his mouth showing how disgusted he was.

Now she disgusted him, yet when he had followed her around she had been his princess. She sought her mother's attention again as tears slid down her smooth cheeks and savagely wiped them off with the palm of her hand. What a mess this was all turning out to be. Her Nana would have brought Jeffrey to account. Made him do right by her, but she was long gone to be with the Lord.

Had she been so naïve she had failed to see the signs before. Jeffrey's callous way when she didn't want to be intimate with him. How like a petulant three year old, he had told her they were girls more beautiful than her willing to be with him. The act that had produced this child that they wanted to get rid of hadn't been at all appealing; rather it had been demeaning as he took her virtue in his father's car. An outsider would always be that, an outsider, since her yearning heart had tricked her into thinking, finally she could be a part of a good and loving family. The Pastor always commended his children for being good and exemplary. All that was just a veneer as Jeffrey the Pastors son turned out to be the opposite. He sweet talked her into falling in love with him and dumped her when it suited him. Fear had driven her not to tell her mother or any adult when she found out she was pregnant. Rather she made a makeshift corset so it wouldn't show while Jeffrey promised to stand by her and inform his parents. They were good parents after all, so they would understand the plight of the two lovers, allow them to get married and live happily ever after.

She believed him, his lies, fake promises, all of it, hook, line and sinker. She even had a mental image of being impeccably dressed in the suits and wide brimmed hats that ministers' wives loved so much. She would be extolled for being the epitome of womanhood, like the

Proverbs 31 woman and an entourage of well-dressed ushers will always be at hand to accompany her to the seat next to the Pastor, her husband. What a fool she was, living in fool's paradise. Having been on the sidelines all her life, when Jeff painted the beautiful picture of the life they would have, she had gladly grabbed it with her whole being.

Her family consisted of her mother and her. No father figure apart from of course Jeffrey's father who happened to be her mother's employer. So what he was offering appealed to her senses and emotions more than anything else. Except in an instant he snatched the dream away. She chided her heart for being so gullible and for being taken in by a trickster masquerading as a lamb. The minister extolled his son so much. Jeff was different, he was their peer educator, their leader and respected ladies. Bah, lies, all lies. She stared at her slight bump, loathing her body as usual. Finally her body had given up over the abuse of having a corset tied tightly around the midsection. For some days she had been feeling faint and ignoring thinking it will pass. Falling was rather a frequent occurrence in church when the pastor ministered so nothing had seemed out of the ordinary when she fell in a faint.

The lady ushers had merely carried her to the room at the back where she would be attended to by a female minister. Mrs. Williams who ministered to the ladies had reached out to make her comfortable by loosening her clothes and such was her shock when she saw the corset tightly wound around her midsection. At further inspection she came to the conclusion that their choir lead singer was pregnant. This would be a scandal, considering Beth had been leading congregants in praise and worship while fornicating and going against what they stood for. Beth was revived by the old lady and clutched at her dress when she realized the zip had been opened at the back and the corset loosened. Her bump was more pronounced and she sobbed at the realization that her secret was out. Mrs. Williams coaxed her to tell her who the father of the child was and such was her shock when Beth announced it was Jeffrey the pastors' son. Her mother was called, the other deaconesses, women who made up the board in their church, Mrs. Matthews, Brice and off course Wilson who happened to be Jeffrey's mother.

The normal practice in such a situation was punishment by stepping down from any leadership position held. Beth being the lead singer in the choir was meant to step down with immediate effect, while Jeffrey also did the same. An announcement would be made by the minister as the couple would be made to stand in front of the congregants and apologize for not walking uprightly as they were meant to. This served as a warning to other youths, to always conduct themselves in a proper manner.

Terminate, the word kept on ringing in her mind. She was a tiny young lady and so was her tummy. Her pregnancy couldn't be terminated. It was far too gone along for that, except the women didn't know since they didn't ask. She heaved a weary sigh as Mrs. Williams was still staring at her and waiting for her to decide between the two judgments passed. "I...I ..will not terminate the pregnancy" she managed to stutter as she gazed her mother's way. "I can't....Jeff is lying, he is indeed the father of this child I am carrying. I have known only him." She felt hurt, dejected and hoped that this whole discussion would come to an abrupt end as she grew wary of having to explain her actions to the women who were already judging her. Mrs. Wilson scoffed, "How do we know girl that my son is the father to that bastard you are carrying. We called him and he denied it. Who are we to believe in all this? I know my son very well and he is not the type to trifle around with a girl. Every relationship he has been in, he is always honest about it and informs me. How come he has never mentioned you?"

She stared at Beth disapprovingly as Beth clutched tightly to the armrest until her knuckles turned white. She could feel her eyes contemptuously rack over her body clad in a plain purple doll dress that once had belonged to Jeffrey's sister and her best friend Joan. Mrs.

Wilson wondered if this was punishment for being kind and taking in mother and daughter.

The other women nodded in agreement as the Jeff they knew was a good boy and this good for nothing maid's daughter had bitten more than she could chew. "For your own information girl, Jeff has been seeing Dora the pastor's daughter from our other branch and they are planning to wed soon. Who is putting you up to this hmmm?" Mrs. Wilson continued as she glared at the blonde girl who barely looked old enough to be an expectant mother. Beth gulped in more air as Mrs. Wilson was being the passionate defender for her son's misdeeds and would gladly box her to reason. Already she had edged to the end of the seat. "Mom," she whispered tentatively, pleading with her eyes and willing her to rise from her stupor, "Believe me, it's Jeff. You can't let them do this to me...."

There wasn't a need for her to finish that statement as Ellen had just heard enough. She had been holding her emotions at bay and listening to everything that was being said. She could feel her heart pounding and the fury churning up in her belly as it rose up and consumed her. For the first time she glared at all the women, having read between the lines to what Mrs. Wilson was insinuating, in that she was the one who had influenced her daughter to lie. Her pumpkin did not lie easily. She had brought her up in the Lord. She wasn't a manipulator. She had been shocked that Beth hadn't told her of her predicament but had hid the pregnancy from her. But now hearing Mrs. Wilson rant and rave, she wondered if Beth had feared her reaction would be the same in that she would not believe her. "Don't you dare accuse my daughter of being loose; I have raised her well in the Lord and have taught her to respect people" she stated with an edge to her voice as gasps of shock from the other ladies could be heard. What was wrong with these women, she wondered as they ganged up on a defenseless girl. "I thought by now a reasonable resolution to this problem would have been reached in which my history is not brought to the forefront. Do you really think I would do such a despicable thing like put her up to this?"

The women were now gawking at her as if she had suddenly grown another head. Mrs. Williams's eyes now looked like saucers as she gaped in amazement at the impudence she was witnessing. Ellen grabbed hold of her daughter's arm and hauled her to her feet "Come on pumpy, we should go. For women who profess to hold to the highest values in honoring God, your behaviour is appalling. You are all murderers." Mrs. Matthews shifted and lowered her eyes to the floor embarrassed while Mrs. Wilson stood up and screeched, "You see that, all of you. She is a bad tree and the fruit definitely did not fall far from it. Look at her. I will not let you destroy my son's future. I will make sure that the community shuns you." Ellen and Beth were of the same petite frame while Mrs. Wilson was bulky, hence as she lunged at mother and daughter, Beth shrieked, while her mother stood resolutely as the other women managed to hold Mrs. Wilson from doing them bodily harm. "We should have done so when you fell pregnant for a stranger 18 years back, but no, we did the Christian thing. Look what it has brought us".

Ellen was still pulling at Beth undeterred by the big woman as they left the room, not even listening to her tirade. They hadn't noticed that so much time had passed while they were holed up in the room. When they came out, it was already dark as they trudged to their house behind the church. Ellen had been a maid for the pastors' family ever since she fell pregnant and did not finish her education. She knew that Beth was a good girl and different from her in many ways. She on the other hand was once a rebellious teen and against her better judgment hooked up with a man who came to their town for the church conference that had been held for the youths. She only knew his name, Richard Reynolds.

That encounter cost her everything. She accepted her fate over the whole issue and retreated into a shell after that. Her widowed mother always strong in her beliefs didn't offer the option of termination to the pregnancy. Instead she got her employed at the pastor's house as a maid at the age of sixteen. Her mother wished much more for her than being a maid as she was, instead she went and blew the whole thing off.

Eighteen years down the line, her daughter did the same. She imagined her mother cackling with glee and stating that whatever was happening was inevitable. At the same time, she had told her that she would never know the love of a parent until she had her own child. She was surprised that she had voiced out the way she had to those women. She definitely would protect her young no matter what might come her way. No one was going to abuse her daughter like that while she was still alive. They were panting as they arrived, got into their house and Ellen quickly locked the door.

They gazed at each other and for a second, Beth caught a glimpse of her mother's once rebellious nature that her granny once spoke of. At the time she didn't believe a word and Beth concluded those were just the ramblings of an old woman. Uncontrollable laughter issued from the two women, accompanied by tears as her mother slumped dejectedly onto the bed. Beth rushed to her side and hugged her. "I am sorry mom, I should never have let this happen. Knowing your history and how you struggled to give me the best of everything. I am so- - so- - sorry". Their bodies shook with heart wrenching sobs as they cradled and comforted each other.

Finally Ellen disentangled her arms around her daughter and sniveled. "We should pack; I don't think will be welcome here after all that has taken place." She could see the tortured expression on her daughters face as she felt guilty. "Don't worry pumpy" she pulled on a smile and tilted Beth's face so she could look into her eyes. "It is well."

"But mom, where will we go?"

"I have a relation who stays in Graceland, that's a good place to start afresh." She wiped off Beth's tears and turned to the task at hand of packing up their things. She looked around at what used to be their home. The bedroom was huge while the kitchen was smaller in size and one person was meant to be in it at a time since they wasn't much space to move around. She would inform her friend to sell their furniture and the money would help them as they transitioned. Courtney was good at selling second hand things and she knew how to find the buyers quickly. She took her phone and texted her. She doubted very much that Mrs. Wilson will take kindly to seeing their faces all the time, when such a huge elephant hung over their heads. Her employer might have been married to a pastor but she wasn't saintly at all.

Beth watched her mother pack up and felt guilty for bringing such trouble in her life, she didn't deserve all this. She thought back to how her granny used to say that one should never cry over spilt milk and managed to push aside the overwhelming need to give into more tears. She got up and started helping her pack. "How far along are you?" her mother asked as she packed the clothes in a suitcase. There was a slight pause. "Beth" her mother asked softly. She grabbed her hand and settled down with her, "How far along are you?" Beth lowered her eyes to the floor, ashamed for having hidden the truth for such a long time. "Eight months." For the first time her mother stared at her shocked before she burst out laughing. Beth stared at her sheepishly not having expected that reaction. "Well pumpy, you got one over me. I was four months along when your granny discovered it."

"Moom"

"Come on it is done, stand up and pack before they chase us out." She was chuckling as she went back to work at the same time apprehensive over how their life would turn out. She hoped that Beth would not go through what she went through. Since Jeffrey had denied his involvement with Beth, she was going to make sure that he never came in contact with her daughter and manipulated her again, before she knew it, Beth will be tending to a second child. Over her dead body will that happen?

"Do you think your relation will take us in?" Beth asked worriedly. "Rosemary once invited me for a visit during the time when you were registering for your exams. Its time I took her up on her offer."

"Is Graceland a nice place?" Beth was rambling as she wanted to forget about what they were doing. "I guess it is what would you expect of a place full of farming lands and where one has to climb mountains to get reception. According to Rose it's a safe haven and a good place to start afresh." For a second Beth stared at her mother incredulously having forgotten that she was the one who had exiled them to such a fate. "Pack up, that's the last of the bags right" her mother stated before they picked up the bags and left the house.

The night was silent and they were relieved that the pastor's wife hadn't bothered to come to their quarters to bodily throw them out. They both knew that the next day would be a different matter. Before she could step out from the church gates, Ellen couldn't resist the urge to get into the church for the last time. Her prayer was that God guide them in their path and not forsake them now in their hour of need.

Beth also knelt down. She couldn't shake off the guilt that she felt. What had she done? Her mother had tried by all means to bring her up well and this is how she repaid her. She prayed, "God, I know my mother has more faith in your goodness and mercy than I have. I feel guilty and it is justified since I did things my way and not yours. Your word confines sex to the marital bed and it serves me right what I got in return for transgressing your law. I ask you to forgive me for doing things my own way. Please be with us and guide us. Make my path straight and for this unborn child to have a steady home. I promise to work hard from now on and will do things your way and no longer mine. I promise to serve you fully, if you could just take me from this whole mess I have done. Amen." She heaved out a heavy sigh after the prayer and stood up before walking out from the life she knew. Her mother was already waiting outside for her. The bus terminus was a short distance from the church. They noticed that one of the buses was about to be full and depart. Getting in, it immediately set off for the train station. It was when they were in the train that they finally settled down, relieved from the events that had taken place and fell asleep.

Chapter 1

BETH DRAGGED OUT A long heavy sigh while she stared outside the window at the rain that was slowly falling, wondering on what to do. She was bored and her huge bulk didn't help matters. She was now at Graceland and as her mother had stated before, it was a good place to make a fresh start. The community was far removed from the events happening in the world as people lived their lives and went on about their duties with smiles always on their faces. Everyone knew each other. The small town boasted of malls, convenience stores, gaming halls, cinemas and so much more. They were so many activities to be done that kept young people from being idle. Outside town, huge acres of farming lands could be seen as farmers went on about their duties so as to provide produce to the markets in town. They was a beach where youths could be found frolicking around on a good day, while fisherman made a living out of the different fish they managed to catch in the river. She heaved out another sigh and Rosemary who had been knitting finally put aside her things and glared at her good humoredly.

"What is it now Bethy girl?" she asked cocking her brow in the process and bringing about a smile on the young lady's face.

"Nothing just bored."

Her mother's aunt turned out to be just like her grandmother and she loved her to bits. She had deeply etched laugh lines on her face, evidence of one who enjoyed and took life at its stride. Her soft gray hair reminded Beth of her grandmother a lot as she could be found plaiting the woman at times as they chatted about everything.

Rosemary had gladly taken in the duo, offered them a roof over their heads and a fresh start. She had chided Ellen over taking long to visit her while she winked at her grandniece and advised that she would look for a good male suitor for her to her horror. Having been widowed three years after she got married, Rosemary never contemplated taking the marriage route again but rather built upon the plans that she and her husband had made prior. She didn't have any children and was content in owning a farm with a couple of loyal workers. On a small scale she had a few products that came from her farm, a Granny brand which included peanut butter, orange marmalade, flour and orange juice. The old woman was successful and hence decided to take Ellen under her wing and teach her the trade. For the mean time she had advised her relations to rest and hence Ellen was making friends in the community while her daughter's bulge prevented her from making such a progress. The bulge apparently didn't matter to Rosemary since she had already lined up a few potential suitors, starting with David who met Beth while she was out shopping for baby clothes with her grandaunt. Beth had been standing a bit further away while the young man's eyes kept straying to her as he spoke with Rose. She smirked; having noticed the young man's interest and was more than willing to point out, "Dave my dear boy, she is already knocked up. If you need a ready-made family, she is good to go." Beth had wished for the ground to open up and swallow her, while she could see Dave's embarrassed expression. Her aunt went on to pat her back after he left, softly stating to her horror, "Will get you married soon Bethy, in these parts they are honorable young man willing to do what your beau failed." Apart from that embarrassing scene she rather enjoyed her outing with her grandaunt. They got into Baby world and Beth glossed over everything as she moved and picked out what her baby would need.

Graceland was indeed paradise, she thought as she trudged around from shop to shop even spotting costume shops with fairy tale costumes for hire. The one downside as her mother mentioned was the communication to the outside world. She could easily communicate locally yet bad reception was the norm when it came to contacting the outside world. Having a T.V. appeared to be rare as most of the resident homes boasted of huge libraries with a wide range of books. The print industry strived and fared well in the town.

Beth cleared her mind from her thoughts and listened to what her aunt was saying. "Why not visit Lisa" Beth grumbled at that since her mother and aunt appeared to have assumed that she will get along with Lisa as she was an expectant mother also. She was the Senior Pastor's daughter in law. Ellen apparently had a knack of attracting and befriending minister's wives. She was now friends with the senior pastors wife where her aunt fellowshipped. They instantly hit it off and expected their daughters to do the same. Lisa and Elizabeth were two poles apart like night and day. Beth was still a young girl at heart who delighted in having fun. If not for her bulk she would have made use of the gaming facilities offered. She wasn't comfortable with exposing her bulk swimming with the rest so she stayed away from the river. Lisa on the other hand was domesticated.

All she thought about was homely stuff, like knitting, sewing, preparing for the baby and gardening. Beth on the other hand didn't see the need to do so; she could just buy everything in the shop. Her arms already ached from being prodded by the needle as Lisa had tried to teach her to sew. "Lisa is not my friend granny. We are just too different."

Rose rolled her eyes and suggested slowly as if addressing a three year old, "Why don't you get a book to read then, or check if Rob managed to make a match for you." *They she goes again*, Beth thought as Rose spoke about marriage. Robin was Lisa's husband and just like his father, had chosen the path of ministry. He had jet black hair and a cute dimple on the cheek when he smiled. She was struck by his brown kind eyes that seemed to have long lashes like that of a lady. He was broad shouldered, lithe when he moved and smiled a lot, while his wife was slender like her, dark haired and usually scowled at him as he tended to be friendly with everyone. The bronzed tan of his skin was evidence to his outgoing nature as he was an outdoor man. She could see by the way he looked at his wife that he was so much in love with her and at times Beth found herself wondering how it could have turned out if she had made a better choice before.

Lisa appeared to be sullen at times and of a sour disposition making Beth wonder how the two ever got married in the first place. Who was she to take note on a mismatched couple when she had made a mess of her life thinking that a man loved her when he didn't? She sighed again when she thought of Jeffrey and wondered what he was doing now, having gotten rid of the pest known as Elizabeth Martins out of his life. "Will you stop that?" Rose bellowed startling Beth from her thoughts. Before she could reply, the door was opened and a cool fresh breeze swept into the room.

"What is going on, I could hear you shouting from the gate" Ellen commented as she came into the house. She was glowing and Beth could swear that her mother had put on a bit of weight as her cheeks looked plumper and ruddier. She marveled at how young, beautiful and carefree she looked with her blue twinkling eyes and brown hair as compared to her daughter's pale one. Funny she had never thought of her mother in those terms before, but here she was looking young as after all she was just thirty four years old. Instead of looking for a match for her daughter, she should be finding a man for herself; Beth thought and chuckled in her heart imagining her walking down the aisle.

"Your Bethy girl keeps on sighing," Rose gritted out eliciting a chuckle from Ellen. It had stopped raining hence she rushed to the kitchen and came back to the living room with a khaki paper in hand. "Be a sweet heart pumpy and give this to the pastor, he is waiting outside."

Rose raised her brow inquiringly while Ellen explained, "It's the pumpkin seeds meant for Tina, totally forgot about them when I went for a visit. So she sent her son to collect them for her." Beth heaved a sigh before she stood up, while Rose rolled her eyes and her mother chuckled. She took the paper and walked out avoiding some puddles as she breathed in the cool fresh air. Her mother peeped through the door and hollered "Maybe you might also go out to town with him and his wife" making Beth cringe out of embarrassment. She didn't want to intrude on the young couple and be a spare wheel. "Hey Beth" the couple greeted in unison as she reached their car and gave the paper with the pumpkin seeds to Lisa. "Your mom was saying you are tired of being cooped up in the house, so we actually came for you."

"I hate to intrude." She was mortified as the women in her family kept on sticking her up to Lisa like an unwanted rag doll while Lisa managed to produce a smile that didn't reach her eyes. Beth could detect a hint of irritation on her demeanor, Yet she politely replied, "It's okay" before she scooted over in the pickup truck for Beth to get in. Rob winked at her putting her more at ease.

"If you are sure about this."

"We are" the couple replied in unison.

Beth slid in and shut the door to the car almost laughing as she looked at the picture they made. Lisa was six months pregnant while she on the other hand looked like one who might give birth anytime. She longed to sleep properly as she no longer could sleep on her tummy. She was struggling to bath herself. She didn't know that being pregnant could be that uncomfortable. They finally reached town and got off from the car to the deli that sold tasty burgers and pies she had grown to love so much. Mr. Wilkinson the owner of the small deli would at times add an extra burger or pie to Beth's delight if he was behind the counter when she visited the place. Someone called Lisa and when she turned as they were about to get into the small deli, Lisa waved back and excused herself leaving her husband standing awkwardly with Beth. Rob grinned before asking, "Shall we? She might take a while."

"Ok."

They got into the deli which had a few customers in it. Beth settled down and sighed. "Comfortable," Rob asked eliciting a giggle from her on how concerned he seemed. "Very."

"So what would you like?" He watched her literally contemplate on what to eat. Having a pregnant wife made him rather a pro on their eating habits. He could swear her face was lighting up over every item as she failed to make up her mind. "Ok, I will settle for the beef burger, French fries and pulpy orange juice."

"Anything else," Rob chuckled to her horror as she wondered if she had ordered too much. "Nope."

He got up and walked to the counter. It was surprising that she felt more comfortable in Robin's company than Lisa's. He seemed more approachable and accommodating, when she could swear that Lisa looked at her disdainfully as if she was a pesky pest. She couldn't explain that to Aunt Rose, so she had settled for the other explanation on why she couldn't be friends with her.

He came back with the tray laden with food having ordered for his wife also. Went back and came back with a large sized box of the four season's pizza that he handed to her. "I know you want it," he smirked as she laughed. He was such a considerate friend and she liked him. Her mouth was salivating over the thought of eating the pizza at night as she tended to make the food rounds in the middle of the night. The deli strived on quality and quantity and hence as she delved into the food she couldn't help but groan. Her taste buds were somehow enhanced by her pregnancy but she wasn't embarrassed as Robin laughed at her antics.

By the time Lisa came into the deli, Beth was having difficulty breathing and her ribs hurt from listening to Robs jokes. Lisa scowled at the scene. "Are you not joining us love?" Rob asked in surprise as she informed him to change her order to a take away. "I just want to go home" she sulked and turned to leave since she knew her husband would follow. Rob who was used to her tantrums winked at Beth and took the food to the counter for them to pack up. Beth had quite enjoyed his jokes. She was relieved, having been done with lunch and was slowly sipping on the juice before surly Lisa took the fun out of their chat. "Shall we?" Rob rushed to her side and helped her stand as she rolled her eyes at how concerned he appeared to be. "There is no need for all this fuss, you know that." She had an image of surly Lisa huffing and impatiently waiting outside. He took the box and held it for her as they moved out and nodded at the other customers.

"News flush you are pregnant. Someone needs to make you feel special at this time. By the way you should tell your granny that I found you a husband."

Beth glared at him, wishing she could pinch him as his grin widened. "Not you also" she growled. "I am off men for life. Do me a favour and keep him as far away from me as you possibly can. Unless if his very old with one foot already in the grave and extremely rich. Then we can talk." She smirked as she watched his horrified expression change to one of mirth as he laughed, not taking her seriously at all. "Ha-ha, very funny." She sighed; already her mother and aunt didn't believe that she was off men for life, as they kept on pointing out that the hormones would soon kick in after the birth of the baby. She had learnt her lesson; she was off sex for good. Her ribs still hurt from laughing and she was rather surprised since her back suddenly ached also. As they drew near the entrance, she felt a trickle and stared in horror on the floor while Rob walked ahead oblivious of the fact that his laughing partner wasn't on his side. Lisa nodded her head and motioned with her arms, "who are you talking to?" and watched Rob turn to his side. He looked back, only to see Beth still standing on the door in a daze. He handed over the supplies he had been carrying before rushing back to her. "Halloo" he called as he walked towards her. So much for trying to talk some sense into Beth on relationships, she didn't hear a word to any of it since she had remained behind. Beth could at times be weird, he thought. He rather enjoyed her company and her sense of humor and he knew the young man he had in mind will be kind to her and treat her well. The youths in his church kept on talking about the city girl. Good on the eyes and friendly. The pregnancy didn't matter to them as more of them were willing to take her on and her unborn child. How could it matter after all, when men appeared to be more as compared to women? Graceland was a place for farmers and it was only in recent years that they started building malls, cinemas and shops so as to accommodate the females and provide the luxury they required. He knew she would be horrified if he told her on how many of the young men had approached him so he could make the introductions.

As he drew nearer to where she stood, he frowned, raising a questioning brow in the process. "Beth." He reached for her hand which she immediately snatched back. "Beth, what's going on?" She looked horrified and embarrassed at the same time.

"My water just broke." That's when he noticed a small puddle. "I don't know if I should pant, scream or laugh" she remarked eliciting a chortle from him. "If I move, will my baby fall?" that's when he roared out with laughter realizing why she didn't want to leave the spot. "Come on pumpy," he stated using the nickname he always heard her mother call her by. "The baby will not fall. Are you in pain?"

"Slightly."

She managed to move finally as he helped her walk. "What is going on?" Lisa asked glaring at them. She was tired of waiting for the two who appeared to be goofing around. She noticed that Beth was clinging to her husband's arm as if her life depended on it while sweating profusely and panting through gritted teeth. "Beth is in labour" Rob answered to her annoyance. *Great now we have to take her to the hospital.* Lisa thought as she said with concern on her face "I hope you are not in pain." She might not have liked the girl that much but she didn't want her to be in pain. Everyone around her was overly concerned about her which irritated her to no end.

With the way Rob had been acting around Beth, one would think he was the father to her unborn child and his attitude was beginning to annoy her. She huffed and got into the car. "It's going to be a bumpy ride," Rob commented as he made her more comfortable at the back of the truck and got into the car. As he had advised, Beth kept on bracing herself as he drove like a maniac. *The nerve of the man, pretending to be calm while he encouraged me to walk*, she thought. In no time, they arrived at the hospital and when she was about to protest as he swiftly carried her, he shouted to her mortification, "woman in labour."

She finally realized why he was such good friends with her aunt considering the huge age difference. They were definitely birds of the same feather when it came to embarrassing the hell out of her.

Chapter 2

LISA REACHED OUT TO her husband who was slowly pacing the waiting room at the hospital making a path on the carpet and tentatively asked "Can we go home now?" His hair was ruffled since he had raked his fingers through it as he waited. It irritated Lisa to no end as he appeared to be oblivious to how tired she felt. He stared at her as if he hadn't heard what she said before remarking, "Don't you want to make sure that she is fine? Thought she was your friend."

She scowled, "she is not, and your mother foisted her on me so I could show her around the town, that's it. Why does everyone keep on saying she is my friend?" She could hear her husband draw out a heavy sigh, before he pulled her to a chair and settled down next to her. "Can we at least wait for her mother and grandmother, it's the least we can do. The poor girl needs someone by her side as she goes through..."

"I am tired of all this poor girl stuff, Beth this, Beth that, from everyone around me. Why do you keep on acting as if she is the only girl who was lied to by a man? " She yelled. Already Rob was staring at her disapprovingly at her outburst. Usually he didn't mind when she sulked or made some demands yet at this particular outburst, his mouth became a straight line as he warningly stared at her, "Lisa." Before he could speak further two women burst into the waiting room. "How is she?" they asked in unison, concern evident in their faces. "She is fine, no need to panic" he assured them. "Thank you so much for bringing her to the hospital," Ellen stated and hugged Lisa in the process. Rose placed the bag with the necessary things Beth would need after the delivery and sighed out loud as she settled down on the chair.

Edging back again to her husband and looking hurt Lisa whispered, "There are here, can we go." Rob scowled about to retort on how inconsiderate she had suddenly become when Rose softly stated with understanding in her eyes, "Thank you for the help both of you. We can take it from here. You need to take care of your wife's health also." She winked and watched the young couple leave after hugging her and Ellen.

"What was that all about?" Rob finally asked when they were in the car. "In case you didn't notice, I am also pregnant and I am tired" she sulked as she pointed at her chest and turned away from him. Rob looked at his beautiful wife and noticed she did indeed look tired. He pulled her into his arms and apologized, "Sorry honey, for not having paid any attention to you. Will you forgive me." She huffed as he kissed her on the top of her head, not at all deterred by her attitude. He missed his cheery Lisa as the pregnant Lisa tended to be irritable almost all the time. One day she would be all sunny and loving and the next dark and broody. A sudden thought occurred as he pulled her away from him and stared into her eyes, "Are you jealous of Beth?"

"Am not." His grin widened as she attempted to cover her reddened cheeks. He roared out with laughter and at the end she stopped her attempts, giggled as she thought on how absurd it sounded when voiced out loud that she was jealous of Beth. She knew Rob loved her ever since they were young. "Oooh love, you shouldn't" he smirked as he continued holding her in his arms and inhaled her lavender scent. "You are the love of my life; no one will ever take your place."

"Pinky swear," she giggled eliciting a chuckle from him as he tapped at her small finger with his. "Thank you" She kissed him on the cheek and settled properly on the seat. "Can we go home now?" She surely was relentless. "Your wish is my command my queen," he stated and put the key into the ignition before starting the car.

BETH GRUMBLED AS THE light streamed in from the window and she tried to shut it with her hands. Finally she gave up the fight of curling back to sleep and slowly opened her eyes. She could hear the voice of a male person cooing and her eyes widened as she saw a nicely dressed young man cradling her son in his hands. Jeff when and how, she wondered. He was dressed in slim fit navy blue slacks with a blue shirt and matching waistcoat. Her son seemed tiny as he held the head in the palm of his hand and the other cradled his whole tiny body. He had been pacing around, but when he heard the rustle of the sheets, he turned and moved towards her. Love could be seen in his eyes and pride. "Bethy you have made me proud, we have a son." He placed the baby in her arms before he leaned over and kissed her on the forehead. She inhaled his musky cologne, staring at how smartly dressed he was. Jeffrey was always formal and loved suits. She couldn't believe that this was all happening and that he had finally come around. She smiled and was surprised when he knelt down on the floor looking remorseful. "What's wrong love?"

"Please forgive me Beth for hurting and denying you." A slight pain passed across her breast as she watched tears roll down his cheek. "Shhh," she silenced him and whispered, "All is forgiven, and you are here now." He smiled, stood up and sat next to her, giving her a hug before whispering, "I love you." The baby started crying then and wouldn't keep quiet as she shushed him. Finally he quieted down and she huddled in Jeffrey's embrace except it wasn't Jeff but the hard pillow on the hospital bed. She opened her eyes widely as she realized where she was. Rob was pacing the room, holding the baby in his arms, shushing him and very much a contrast to Jeffrey. His dark hair was ruffled up as if by the wind and he wore blue jeans and a checkered shirt. "Hey" he turned and greeted. "You are awake." She nodded and watched him come over to her bed. She was still disoriented wondering where his wife was. "Congratulations you have a bouncing baby boy," he chuckled and stretched out his arm to handover the child to the mother to be fed. Beth hesitated as she regarded her son who looked so like the father. Every word of rejection he ever spoke to her came with full clarity, the lies, the empty promises and the betrayal.

She didn't want the child and she found herself loathing the fact that he had survived. "Beth" Rob raised his brow confused and also seeing the hurt in her eyes. "Don't, please" he pleaded. "This child did nothing to you. Don't reject him, please. You are all he has got." She stared at him incredulously, wondering how he could see right through to what she was thinking. "Congratulations my pumpy" Ellen shouted rushing into the ward oblivious of having interrupted anything. She hugged her daughter and took her grandson from Rob. Rose, Lisa and Tina followed after bringing along the noise and laughter with them. The elders gushed at the baby while Lisa smiled and congratulated her. They came bearing gifts which they handed to her with flourish. Beth stared at Rob who appeared to have a hurt expression on his face on behalf of the son. "Thank you" she muttered looking away from him and meeting the same brown long lashed eyes on his mother's face as she smiled.

"It's nothing dear. You are family" Tina grinned and hugged her. The baby started crying and this time, her mother who had been holding him, shoved him into her arms. She gazed at her son as Rob coughed and excused himself. "What are you waiting for?" Rose asked with a raised brow as her niece kept on staring at the bawling child. "Get to work Bethy girl, motherhood has arrived," she chuckled before Beth finally realized her reality and attended to the child. She peered at the tiny pink mouth as she guided her son to her nipple. The warmth that overcame her when he placed his tiny warm moist mouth flooded her with tears. "Beth are you ok?" her mother asked alarmed while the other women were busy conversing with each other. "I am" she finally muttered.

Chapter 3

BETH WAS FEELING EXHAUSTED as she hadn't been sleeping properly lately because baby Ryan kept her awake all night. It has been two months after his birth and she was getting used to the pains of motherhood as the joy part seemed like a myth to her. Her mother and aunt were always cackling with glee as they watched on Ryan keeping her on her toes, while pointing out a husband would solve all her problems. Then she would be forced to take care of a husband also when she was barely managing with her son.

Three weeks after she had Ryan, Rob came for a visit and invited her to her favorite deli. She was still craving salty food and had gladly accepted the invite, not realizing she was walking into a trap. She was rather happy that surly Lisa wasn't with him. It will just be him and her, having a good time, except it served her right for having such ugly thoughts. Her mother had been more than helpful in picking what she could wear. She should have read the signs then but nope, she was still the gullible Beth who took things at face value. They had set off for the deli, Rob being courteous as ever as he opened doors for her. He rather looked handsome and she hoped she wasn't falling for the good pastor since he was already engaged elsewhere.

It was when she spotted the young man he last spoke about that everything fell into place. It was a blind date. She had nearly run off from there except Rob held her hand firmly and slowly led her to her date who stood up and welcomed her. He was beaming. How she had wished to kick Robs feet under the table. He said a few words of introduction before standing and leaving the two to get acquainted. She sighed resolved to her fate as she listened to what Charles was saying. Charles Thompson was rather a lively young man who kept on droning on and on about himself.

How she longed for her sweet bed, even being with cranky Ryan had appealed to her more that the handsome self centred man who kept on reminding her of her ex. At last he had looked sheepishly at her and apologized since apparently he was nervous and wasn't used to blind dates. She had smiled and answered his every question afterwards as she toyed with her food, no longer craving the salty food after all.

Pastor Rob was either blind to his friend's faults or was pulling her leg. She had been bored to death while her family convinced her to go on another date with him, after he dropped her off at her house. Always wanting to please and not repeat her mistake, Beth had reluctantly agreed and called him. Yes indeed she would be delighted to go for a second date with him. It turned out to be an improvement as they went to the funfair where she immensely enjoyed playing the different games offered, including riding the roller coaster while she screamed her lungs out. Charles presented with flourish a few fluffy dolls he managed to win for her to her delight. She grudgingly admitted herself that Rob was right in his choice, the outgoing; ready to amuse Charles was fun to be around than the bubbling, nervous, self centred date he had been before. Yet she felt Charles was more of a friend than a husband potential, they just wasn't that spark. That same spark that got her in trouble in the first place, which fizzled out immediately afterwards.

Lisa remained somewhat of her surly friend who would pop in when her husband paid them a visit. Beth used to wonder why she actually came along, as she appeared not to like being in her company. "Beth visitor" Rose hollered from the living room as Beth cringed and Ryan stirred in his crib. She hoped he wouldn't wake up. Good, he was still sleeping. She scowled and almost woke him up so they would both sleep at the same time, than to have him wailing his lungs out at night while she tried to sleep. Tiptoeing from the room, she went downstairs where her aunt was and was shocked at seeing her visitor Lisa settled on the couch and chatting with the old woman. She looked up having heard Beth come into the room and smiled. "Hi Beth."

"Hi Lisa" Beth almost turned to look behind her, suspecting Lisa was grinning at someone else rather than her. Her beautiful eyes twinkled with merriment while Beth suddenly felt gloomy. "Lisa thought you would like to go out to the hair salon than being cooped up in the house," Rose softly spoke as she stared at her niece standing awkwardly in the living room. Beth moved towards the love seat opposite Lisa and settled there before replying. "A bit tired from all the work, maybe some other time" she suggested as Rose shook her head negatively. "You need to get out more Beth. Wait five minutes for her while she changes." She almost screamed at the old woman but resignedly left the room to go and change. Get out more, wasn't that what she had been doing going out with Charles. She wondered on why Lisa seemed amicable. As promised, five minutes later she was in the car and they were heading off to the hair salon. "See you in two hours' time," Rob advised before driving off. As usual he had been the one talking in the car whilst the ladies slotted in one or two words in the conversation. Beth chuckled at that fact wondering if being a pastor made him delight in just hearing his voice. He surely could pull a one man conversation without even realizing it. "Let's get you all made up" Lisa brightly stated and ushered her into the salon. Having settled down, Sharon the hairdresser thumped a catalogue before her where she could choose the hairstyle she wanted. Lisa was more than helpful and Beth was getting rather irked. Not being one used to pretending, she finally blurted out, "why are you being so friendly to me all of a sudden?" They were the first clients so Lisa motioned to Sharon to excuse them for a while before she turned back to Beth and cradled her hands into hers. "I am sorry about always being sullen with you. It's just that I have been going through certain things and took it out on you. Will you forgive me?" Beth slowly nodded relieved that Lisa didn't dislike her. She was further surprised when the older girl hugged her. She yelped when one of Lisa's rings got stuck in her hair. "Sorry love" she chuckled before tugging at it and finally loosening it out. She waved to Sharon who came back. As Beth perused through the catalogue showing the latest hairstyles, Lisa pointed out a hairstyle she thought might suit her. "No. no" Beth chuckled as she didn't want to cut her hair and change its color. "This one is the best," she pointed out as Lisa scowled, "That's how your hair looks like now. Live a little Beth, try out something new" she smirked as Sharon joined in, "I assure you, you will look good in this."

Beth finally gave in and allowed them to cut her waist length long hair. How she wept for it in her heart as she saw the strands falling on the floor. On the upside she rather enjoyed Lisa's company as she regaled her with gossip around town and discovered that Lisa joked much the same way Rob did. She guessed this was the Lisa, Rob fell in love with and not the surly woman she met. "Will you excuse me for a bit? Feeling a bit hungry" Lisa stated as Beth laughed. "What do you need?" Beth ordered a chicken pie and cola before she left.

"ARE YOU READY FOR THE reveal," Sharon asked in her breathy voice after completing the whole works on Beth. Her hair now reached to the shoulders, it was now colored black and also Sharon had made up her face to complement the new look. Beth was still apprehensive as she nervously bit the corner of her lip before replying "I think so."

"You look good love, no need to be nervous," she soothingly stated before turning her to face the mirror. Her eyes were lowered down as her long hair on the floor told her a different story. She heaved a sigh, finally looked up and gasped. This couldn't be her, she thought as she stared in surprise at her heart shaped face, pert nose and luscious lips painted red. The black hair suited her to the nines and for a while she thought she was staring at someone she knew but couldn't put a finger on who it might be. She stood up, still gawking at her expression while Sharon looked on with glee. "You love it right. Wait until Lisa sees you. You look so much like her on the day she graduated, you know," she commented as Beth waved her hand dismissively. Lisa, no ways. Lisa was beautiful and even in her pregnancy she turned heads. She and Rob made a perfect couple with their dark hair and classic good looks while Beth was on the course side.

"Lisa has been gone for a while, do you think she is ok."

Sharon dismissively shrugged her shoulders, "Lisa loves to socialize just like her husband." Beth chuckled at that fact and went on to stare at herself in the mirror. "Don't you think the fringe is long, I mean it keeps on getting into my eyes." Sharon stared at her before stating, "Do this" and flipped her head. "Perfect, flip it like that. That's your first lesson to getting the attention of a man," she sniggered as Beth giggled in return.

She was still standing, being vain as she stared at her face while Sharon put away the mirror when she was engulfed in an embrace from the back. She stood still, stunned for a while before looking up on the mirror "You look lovely honey," Rob commented and heard a fit of coughs coming from Sharon.

Lisa turned except it wasn't her. "Good God, you look like my wife." He was shocked at Beth's transformation since he had never realized how so much alike they looked. "I thought the same and told her" Sharon chuckled. "It's like what people say that a person has a doppelganger somewhere in the world. Meet Lisa's double Beth"

Beth was about to protest when they heard the door open and Lisa got into the salon looking ashen as if she had seen a ghost. *Did she witness the hug?* Beth wondered as Rob rushed to his wife and asked if she wanted to take a seat. "What's wrong honey?"

He was worried about her as she looked out of sorts. She produced a wobbly smile before stating, "Good, Beth is done. Just what I had suspected, you look lovely dear." She smiled at Beth and settled on the chair in order to catch her breath. Rob was being overly concerned as usual as he rubbed her back. She rather enjoyed that, why for a while she had thought he liked Beth more than normal, she wondered.

It was when she saw that same concern over one of the married pregnant women after the service that she realized how stupid she had been. When he had looked up after the woman was well settled and comfortable his expression had darkened as he smiled at her. He loved and desired her and his expression showed. She had gulped in a few breaths as he walked towards her smiling as if he knew what she had been thinking. She felt shy and made a promise that she would tell him that she loved him. Really and truly was madly in love with him. "We can leave now since Beth has received her beauty treatment" she stated as she handed the paper bag with the chicken pie and cola to Beth. "Ryan must be wondering where his mommy is." They left for the car and settled in. Beth still looked worried, wondering if Lisa was fine. "Are you sure you are ok?" and received a squeeze from her hand as an answer to that. Her normal color appeared to be returning hence she sat back and watched the trees swaying as the car moved along.

"Thanks a lot for this." Beth got out of the car and looked appreciatively at the couple. "No problem, when Charles sees you, he will marry you on the spot." Both husband and wife said in unison and laughed while Beth grimaced.

Now Lisa was in the mix of trying to marry her off and she had thought she had an ally. They drove off while she walked to the gate of the house. A photographer happened to be passing by so Beth asked for a pic to be taken. He promptly set up his instruments, took the photos and printed the ones she chose. She thanked and paid him before getting into the house where her mother and aunt yelped when they saw the transformation.

"WHY DON'T YOU DROP me at my parents place? Need to visit them for a while." Lisa asked as she stared outside of the window. She felt content in her husband's company and wondered why she never realized the love Rob had for her. Her mother was right, he was a good man. He grunted and continued driving since her parents' house was the same route with theirs. "Would you like me to wait for you, or you will call when you are done?"

"I will call," she chuckled as he still looked concerned. "By the way Mr. you have a lot more of explaining to do with that hug I witnessed."

He cringed as she laughed, she was rather enjoying it. "I thought she was you." He expected her to throw a tantrum over having suggested that but instead she had a thoughtful look on her expression as she answered, "she does, but I thought more like aunt Celestine." Her face cleared and she smiled brightly as she stated, "I will call you when am done" before kissing him on the lips and getting out of the car. "Love you" he hollered as he loved how she would cringe every time he shouted it at the top of his lungs. She usually shyly said thank you but this time, she turned, smiled her sweetest smile and hollered in the same mild manner he had used, "Love you pastor Robin Parker" before she got into her family home leaving a stunned husband in her wake. That was the last time he saw her alive. Her parents called him having rushed her to the hospital. They were some complications while she gave birth and she didn't make it.

BETH KEPT ON PLAYING the scene of the sweet hug over and over in her head. She wondered what was wrong with her and on being attracted to a married man. *He is married Bethy*, she chided herself as she was consumed with the thought of him. *Have I really sunk this low,* she muttered as she readied for bed. Baby Ryan was sound asleep after being fed as if he knew that her mind was elsewhere and she might not hear him cry. *He is Lisa's husband remember,* she mumbled again and got into her blankets. What was it about Rob that made her think such thoughts about him? He had been nothing but good to her, a good friend and also he loved his wife. He didn't deserve to be saddled with her burdensome attention.

What she needed was a man to keep her focus away from the poor pastor and his marriage. Her mother was right in finding Charles for her. Though she didn't look at him in that manner but more as a friend she would grow to love him at the end, she reasoned. While she stayed as far away as she possibly could from the handsome pastor. That hug had more or less turned her into a woman without her faculties in touch. If his hug could make her this crazy, what more if he became interested in her, which was rather impossible. She knew that Rob wasn't that kind of person. He was different from Jeffrey, he walked the talk. She huddled deeply into her blankets and fitfully fell asleep, having images of her and Rob making out. When she woke up the next morning, it was to the sounds of Ryan crying for a diaper change and feed. She came out of her room after completing her tasks and was shocked to find her aunt and mother not around. She tried calling them and their phones were unreachable. Thinking if they had left for something urgent they would have informed her, she decided to prepare breakfast before she dealt with the daily laundry awaiting her attention. She was done with breakfast when they came into the house.

"Morning, where have you been?" she asked a bit concerned when she noticed their sad expressions. "Will you sit down pumpy?" her mother motioned before she grasped her hand. "What's going on mom" she hoped nothing had happened to Rob. With her wandering naughty mind, maybe she had killed him. Coveting what wasn't hers was a sin.

"Beth it's about Lisa," her mother hesitated before she trudged on. "She is no more love. She had some complications while giving birth. She didn't make it."

Tears streamed down her eyes as she thought about her. *I am sorry Lisa for having such wicked thoughts about your husband while you fought for your life,* her heart cried. "Hush love," her mother comforted her as she bitterly wept.

Chapter 4

EVERYONE HAD LEFT FOR their homes after the funeral as Rob remained behind at the gravesite, lost in deep thought. Losing Lisa hurt a lot and he wondered how he would move on without her. He thought back on the day she finally agreed to be his wife and how elated he was. They had visited her family home for dinner. It was after dinner when Lisa excused herself from the rest and went to the library where she usually retired to, with a novel in hand. Rob remained behind, chatting with the adults and left afterwards to check on her. He had always loved her ever since they were kids and everyone had assumed that they will get married, except Lisa had been acting distant as if she wasn't interested. This was now or never, he was finally going to propose. He thought he heard voices except when he got into their family library she was alone and looked rather flushed as she puckered her sweet lips in annoyance for the intrusion. He had merely smirked and got in further into the library. She noticed his intent and quickly scrambled from the seat trying to get away from him. They had fallen in a bundle of giggles as he tickled her, having caught his prey. "Enough Rob," she cutely muttered, breathless as he stopped and stared into the beautiful hazel eyes before leaning in and kissing her. After they drew apart, he had helped her stand and as they were about to walk to the door, she rushed into his arms. "Lisa what's wrong honey?" he enquired, concerned as she trembled and he wondered what had brought that on. He tilted her head and received a pinch on his arm, as she giggled. "Are you not going to ask me?" "Hmmm, thought you weren't interested, that's the impression I got."

"Well I am." She sulked and stamped her feet as she pointed out that he had taken advantage of her. He had been oblivious to his surrounding but only aware of her as he had swooped in again for another tender kiss. She moaned, drawing closer to him and that's how the shocked parents found them. The pastor advised for them to get married quickly as he didn't want any scandals. A sweet slow kiss and he got a wife. He chuckled at the thought brushing aside a tear as he stared at the cloudless blue sky. Though as time went on and she fell pregnant she had become sullen, yet he remembered Lisa, the one who he had always loved and she loved him back as she gave him her all. He dragged out a ragged sigh, walked away from her gravesite and trudged toward his house that suddenly felt dark and gloomy. She had been laid to rest at their family gravesite. He got into the house and loosened his tie. While his father had been reading a bible verse, a paper had fallen from his which he had picked up and absentmindedly placed back in the bible. He settled down near the fireplace and looked at it, turning it over seeing her neat well rounded handwriting. He ran his hand on it and could almost swear he caught a whiff of her lavender scent. *Dear Diary,* it read as he could hear her sweet voice reciting as she wrote, *today I got the proposal that I needed and I don't know whether I should be elated at the good fortune or weep over my lost love. R will provide me with the perfect life that C can't. Already I have lost so much to C yet I feel drawn to him in more ways than I can count. My mother keeps on pointing out that R is a better match and will never accept C. What should I do? Will a secure life for me and my child without love be enough?* By the time he finished reading his heart felt like it had been ground into a million pieces as it suddenly dawned that she had never loved him. *No it can't be?* He thought as he reread the note. It was a page from her diary. He searched for the date entry since it didn't have one where usually the dates were situated and noticed she had signed off *confused* before putting the date. He realized it was written on the same day he proposed.

"ROB SWEETIE." TINA got into her son's house and alarm set in when she spotted him kneeling near the fireplace, savagely tearing at his bible and throwing the pages into the fire. She knew he hurt yet he had managed to hold his emotions at bay ever since he was informed at the hospital that Lisa was gone. He had seemed like an aloof lonely figure as the rest of the relatives and friends left the gravesite while he remained. She grieved along with him, since she had loved Lisa. She rushed to him and knelt on the floor before she cradled his face as he finally let up and wept. "Hush love," was all she could mutter out of any comforting words to say. "It will all be alright." For a while she let him grieve and patted his shoulders reminding her on when he was young and how he would run to her for comfort.

"Someone needs you now more than ever Rob and you have to be strong for her," she advised, making him aware of his new reality of being saddled with a daughter not at all his. He abruptly pulled away and stood up before stating in a harsh tone, "Keep that thing away from me."

Tina gasped and stood up. "Rob what is wrong with you." She stared at him disapprovingly. It was to be expected that he would blame the child for taking away the mother as irrational as that might sound, but she didn't expect such hatred. She stared at Rob who seemed not only to be angry but enraged. "Your daughter needs you my love," she softly stated as she watched him grimace. "That's her daughter ma and if you knew what's good for you, you would keep her far away from me." He walked away and slammed the door right behind him, leaving a hurt and confused mother in his wake.

Chapter 5

ELLEN CRADLED HER GRANDSON as she unlatched the gate to the pastor's house. Tina was her best friend and she enjoyed the woman's company immensely. She was ushered into the living room by the maid where she settled down and waited. "Hi love," Tina greeted and took Ryan from her. "Do bring tea dear," she motioned to the maid and resumed with her friend. "How is our granddaughter doing?" Tina scoffed? "She is doing quite well apart from having an unconcerned father." There was a slight pause as the maid placed the tray with tea on the coffee table before Tina nodded to her and returned to Ellen. Ellen poured the tea into the cups and added sugar in hers while she poured a lot of milk in Tina's.

"Well you might not believe this but Beth rather acts the same way. As if she is avoiding the child and I am now the parent." Both women chuckled as they thought about their children. "By the way, you had mentioned something about Charles."

"Yes, yes, I was wondering on your thoughts about him." Ellen took a sip of tea before she continued, "He wants to marry my daughter after all."

"Charles is a good upstanding young man, but" she hesitated perking up Ellen's curiosity. "What Beth needs is someone who will encourage her to bond with her son, and Charles might be content with the child staying with you."

"I am sure, he will learn to love the son" Ellen waved her arms dismissively aware that Tina was trying to slot her son into the mix.

A lot of women at church had been approaching her with relationship woes pertaining to their daughters of late when Rob's wife was barely two months in the ground. She rather pitied her friend for the pressure she was receiving as the mother of the newly established bachelor or widower.

"I mean Beth also needs a mother in law who will love her like her own. I have the right person for her in mind. The mother is one of those lively people who just love children and she would not mind at all that Beth has a child. The man, oooh boy is he just handsome, respectful and in due time would love Beth to bits." By the time Tina was through with the attributes Ellen was laughing.

"Pray tell Mrs. Parker," she chortled. "Are you suggesting Rob by any chance?"

Already Tina's eyes were twinkling and full of mirth as she chided herself for not having thought of that before. Rob had been a sore spot lately and didn't seem like one ready to recover from his wife's death. What he needed was a spunky wife who would keep him on his toes and Beth was perfect.

"Well Beth is a good girl; she will do more good to my son since he has drifted apart. Reel him in back to this world." The women cackled with glee as they discussed on how they would bring the two together. Ellen marveled at how things were coming up smoothly. She had misgivings about Charles and Tina's suggestion rather solved her problem over Beth and her grandchild. Both of them will receive love and a secure future. "What if Rob takes advantage of her?" Ellen asked, after listening to what Tina was suggesting.

"I know my son very well, and he wouldn't even hurt a fly even if his life depended on it. I will keep a close watch over the house in case she screamed for help."

"It's not funny" Ellen chuckled as Tina said, "It's either that or will try to catch Rob at another time which is rather impossible. It's been a while since I saw him. He goes to work at the mech shop, visits a bar, drinks a bit, comes back home and back to the normal routine of waking up early before anyone has seen him."

"Great, now I am handing over my daughter to a drunkard," she muttered as her friend sniggered. "Rob will come around."

"MOM, YOU ARE EARLY" Beth remarked as her mother came through the gate while she removed the clothes from the line. Bruce the driver waved and left.

"Well Tina is out of sorts, worried about her son, so didn't have much to talk about with her. Am rather relieved that you met a good young man like Charles but I couldn't share this good news with her since Rob is going through a crisis."

She got into the house and walked towards the bedroom where she laid Ryan in his crib before going back to the kitchen and settling down on the chair.

"I am sure Rob will come around, his moaning his wife after all." Beth got into the kitchen and switched on the water for a cup of coffee. "It's been two months now, as much as it might seem cruel, he has moaned long enough, he has a child to think about now." She rubbed her chin as she thought over the matter hoping her daughter would take the bait. "With the way he was so quick to look for a husband for you, he is in a better position of finding a wife since he knows a lot of single women. Other girls are even flocking towards his mother's house, making themselves indispensable."

Beth kept quiet but nodded her head as she prepared the coffee before she handed one mug to her mother, took the other one and settled down. She thought of the young women who were rather transparent when it came to wanting to catch for themselves the widower. They were too eager in plucking Penelope from the granny as soon as she got into church. All the grandmother did was sit and the women took care of Penny's needs. The extent that women will go through to just get married was shocking. Rob was nowhere to be seen after the shocking announcement he made about stepping down as the junior pastor.

She had met him in town while she was out on her date with Charles. He had dropped a few pounds but still looked handsome and this time hardened. There was just a hard edge about him that appealed to her even more. She surely wasn't normal. The man's wife just died. She was just the same like the women clawing their arms around Mrs. Parker just to prove they could make good daughters in law.

"Mom, about Charles," she tentatively spoke, dreading what she would say. Her mother and Aunt Rose appeared to be happy at the prospect of her getting married to Charles. He spoke to them before he approached her and broached the subject on marriage showing that her first assumption had been right. He was such a self centred man. "I don't think we are well suited." Ellen scoffed at that, "what do you mean Bethy. He will be good for you, you should keep Ryan in mind, and he needs a father, being a single parent is not something to be proud of."

"I know, but I don't love him."

She scoffed at that notion. "Like you loved Jeffrey and look what happened. He denied you on the spot. Just let the adults plan for you. After all you grow to love a person. In no time you will fall in love with Charles."

Just as she had thought, her mother would be a hard nut to crack. "Well you took care of me single handedly."

"I did the best I could pumpy but you know what it feels like to grow up without a father. Are you willing to do that to your son?" Her mother was already tapping on the table with her nail, looking agitated as if Beth would mess up with her good fortune once again. Beth thought on how she had longed to meet her father as she grew up. They was always that persistent yearning of knowing the other half that brought her into the world which was never fulfilled. Her mother was honest with her and spoke about her history and the fact that it was a onetime encounter with a handsome stranger. Beth was never a mistake to her, but rather her turning point as she always felt she would have been worse off if she hadn't fallen pregnant when she did. She had watched her friends come in with both parents at school but that was never her fate. She wondered if her father had been in her life, would she have given in to Jeff's demands. "I don't want that buh"

"No buts, Charles is good for you. If not Charles who is willing to give you the love you deserve, why not settle for some other arrangement of some sort?" That perked up her ears. "Get married to Rob." She stared incredulously at her mother and noticed a twinkle in her eyes. She was joking right. Though her heart had skipped a beat at hearing that, Beth shook her head negatively and whispered, "Rob just lost his wife."

"In ancient times do you know for how long a spouse mourned for their loved one?" Beth shook her head, knowing full well her mother would educate her on that. "One week. As in seven days and the man was free to move on." She winked as she motioned to her hands.

"Mother" Beth gasped smothering a laugh at the same time.

"Mother what? Rob needs a mother for his daughter and you need a father for your son. He is also a good person who will always do right by you."

"Rob is moaning his wife" she protested again, yet this time the wind had been knocked off her sails. "And you are moaning over what could have been. You will be a perfect match" she chuckled, "while we are at it, Tina wanted to have a word with you, so pay her a visit in the evening."

Beth was now staring at her mother suspiciously; she didn't take her mother as one of those who schemed. "What is it; hopefully it's not about marriage?" Her mother stared at her with a hurt expression as she answered "Why would she talk about that? She is worried about Rob and how he doesn't seem to care about his daughter. So she thought you can talk to him. After all he is your friend." She couldn't dispute that fact. She longed to see him and have a long chat with him. Never could she have expected Rob who had been hurt when she almost rejected her son would do so to his own daughter. She wondered if the rumors were true that he was doing much more that moaning his wife. He had started drinking also and getting into a few brawls in the process.

She wouldn't have thought that the former pastor would drop that low and rather pitied him. "Ok, I will go and see her" she stated before she finished her coffee and got ready to prepare their afternoon meal.

"MRS. PARKER," BETH called out as she got into the house. The door stood ajar and she went in. The driver had dropped her off at the pastor's house and immediately left while she knocked on the door. She was welcomed by the senior Parker who informed her that Tina was collecting a few things right across the street. The man looked haggard, having lost a daughter in law and she hoped that they would be happiness to fill the once lively home. Work with the congregants must have doubled also since Rob stepped down and he had been the one doing most of the work.

"Hellooo"

Tina got out of the bedroom and smiled at the young lady. "Welcome. I am just collecting a few items for the baby and we can go." Beth helped her with the box and moved out of the house. "I hate having to walk up and down and Robin isn't helping the situation at all. He is never around."

"Mom had mentioned that you wanted me to talk to him. Where is he?" The mother shrugged her shoulders "Only the Lord knows dear. Thank you for coming I know you have a lot to do than be worrying over my good for nothing son."

Beth nodded her head as they crossed the street to the pastor's house. Rob lived right across his parents' place. Beth was relieved that her chat with Tina wasn't over marriage, but rather her good for nothing son. They got into the house and Tina got the box from her. She came back having put it away as Beth asked. "How's Penny doing?"

"Penny is sweet darling, sleeps throughout" she stated sweetly as she spoke about her granddaughter. "That's the main reason why I called for you. Rob is your friend right." Tina leaned in as if conspiring with Beth over something as she asked. Beth hesitated before she could answer not knowing where their conversation would lead "Y-e-e-s, I would like to think he is"

"Good" the mother nodded. "You are also of the same generation hence you might understand each other more. Please talk to him pertaining to his involvement in his daughter's life. Right now he is more of an absentee father than anything else." Beth stared at Tina who looked concerned over her son. Her mother was right she realized. Tina was so worried over him and wouldn't come up with a marriage thought at all. "But you mentioned that he is not around."

"That is why I am pleading with you dear. If you can wait up for him and talk. I know it is too much to ask from you..." Beth reached out to her hand and said, "I understand its fine." She looked relieved after that and quickly stood up as if she feared Beth might have second thoughts. "Great. Let's ..." before she could complete the statement the maid came into the living room with Penny in her arms. "You are awake" the grandmother cooed, taking her from the maid and indicating for Beth to follow. "You do not know how much this means to me" she stated softly as they moved towards Robs place. "No problem. Glad I could be of help" Beth replied and opened the door for her. They spoke for a little while further as she showed her around the house. Beth humored the pastor's wife as she acted as if she was moving in instead of waiting for Rob in order to talk some sense into him. She left afterwards to her house. Robin hadn't yet returned from where he was. Beth busied herself by preparing a meal and had her supper, while she put his food in the warmer. *Where is he,* she wondered and decided to look for something to read while she waited. Tina had pointed out that the library was at the end of the corridor and the first aid kit in the bathroom. She had found it odd at the time but shrugged it off since she had been cooing over Penny when she mentioned it.

The guest room appeared to be lived in as she spotted a few things lying on the floor here and there. She picked the shirt up, inhaled the spicy scent that was so Rob before she threw it into the washing basket annoyed at the way she was acting. This was a bad idea. Her feet faltered at the door to the master bedroom. She opened the door and stared at the bed that was nicely made up as if no one had slept in it for a long time. Moving further into the room, she rubbed her fingers over the mahogany wood making up his furniture and came back with dust. Was Rob making use of the guest room and no longer sleeping in his on. She walked away from the room and moved towards the library where she found a selection of books. Taking a romantic novel, she moved towards the living room and settled on the couch. She thought back on the kind of person he was before his wife died. Him stepping down as a minister had shocked the community just as much as it had shocked his family. The thought on how he was formerly is the one that had driven her to agree to talk to him. She doubted though that he would pay her any attention seeing he wasn't even listening to his own parents.

She couldn't believe that it had been two months since Lisa died. She should have been afraid in being in the house alone, yet she rather felt comfortable. *Get a grip of yourself Beth*, she chided. She must have dozed off because the next time she woke up, a person was sitting next to her, stroking her hair. "Hey" she softly smiled as she sat up on the couch wondering if this was all a dream as he stared at her with longing in his eyes. Rob dragged out a heavy sigh as he stared at the angel smiling only for him. He hadn't expected such a welcome when he got home. His house was dark and gloomy as his heart was and he avoided it as much as he could. He had managed to get rid of some of the stuff that belonged to Lisa, yet everything felt like a mockery to the life they once shared.

Her betrayal was beyond what he could bear. His only thought had been going to sleep on his couch when he got home as the bedroom reminded him of her. He switched on the lamp to his living room and was taken momentarily aback when he saw Beth lying on the couch. One hand hung limply on the carpet with a novel on the side, while the other lay on her stomach. He could see the rise and fall of her chest as she slept and looked peaceful. He felt himself being drawn to her as a moth unto a flame. He had almost left her in that manner and gone to bed in the guest room, since he was a little bit light headed as drinking had become a daily routine to keep his wandering thoughts at bay. He held her hand and placed it on her tummy with the other one and brushed her hair aside that had covered her face. So like Lisa at the same time not her.

He seemed to be tottering between reality and what wasn't as she opened her eyes and smiled sweetly. For a while he forgot about his pain, the hurt he felt and wanted a taste of the light she appeared to exude. "Hey" he whispered before he kissed her. Beth was taken by surprise as he pried her closed lips and delved in with his tongue deeper into her making her tremble. She moaned protesting at the intrusion while he tenderly stroked her back. The kiss became sweet and tender, no longer intrusive as she sighed and responded back. She wrapped her arms around his neck delighting in how solid and dependable he felt. She had lost count of the time as she reveled in the kiss and how he made her feel. She licked his lips slowly tasting the alcohol on them. *What am I doing?* She wondered as her mind sent out warning bells. He was drunk and he didn't know what he was doing while she on the other hand acted like a sex starved woman. "No" she protested and tried to get away from him, except he stood up and grabbed her before she could flee and pasted a hard kiss on her. "You were always a tease, I know you want this."

She managed to draw away from him as he stared at her with eyes that seemed devoid of recognition. "What are you talking about?" He chuckled before answering; "you must have enjoyed and had your fun when you trapped me into the sham of a marriage, knowing full well that you were pregnant." She gasped as he pulled her back into his arms and savagely kissed her. "Rob you hurting me" she cried while he squeezed her body tighter to him. She needed to get away from him and fast. Suddenly she felt scared of what she had been about to do and how she had led him on. She reached out blindly to the side of the couch as he pushed her towards it while mercilessly plundering her mouth. One swing sent him stumbling, having been caught by surprise as disbelief showed on his face. Through the hazy fog that was settling in, he was able to see a horrified Beth staring at him before he crumbled on the floor and darkness engulfed him.

"I killed him" Beth muttered under her breath as she slowly knelt down and cradled his head. A trickle of blood streamed down his face. She was about to scream when he turned and she heard a sound. Drawing closer, he muttered something and snored. She scowled as she had been about to panic over nothing. He would be angry with her tomorrow when he realized she had hit him with the vase. In no uncertain terms was she going to inform his mother about the little incident? What had got over him, she wondered and chided herself for responding in the wanton manner she had.

It had been so long since she had been loved and held in that way. She was young and her mother was indeed right in saying the single parenthood life wasn't an easy one, especially when it concerned her bodily needs. She had thought they were long dead and Rob appeared to have just hit the right note to awaken them.

She sighed out loud and decided to move him to the couch were he would sleep properly. She was panting out of breath by the time she covered him with a fleece and moved towards the bathroom where she got the first aid kit and cleaned up the wound before putting a band aid on it. For a while she stroked his face as it lay on her lap. Rob was always good to her and seeing him in this state broke her heart. "What happened to you Rob" she whispered, finally shifted and placed his head on the couch before going to the guest room and thought over what he had said.

Chapter 6

ROB OPENED HIS EYES and winced. His head hurt a lot as if he had been hit by a sledge hammer. He groaned further when the events of the day before flooded in like a storm. Beth. He was further appalled by his behavior when he thought about how he had treated her. She sure was a strong woman he thought as he got up from the couch and tottered a bit before he regained his balance.

He grimaced when he realized that the vase that used to be at the side of the couch in the living room wasn't there. So she had hit him with that, no wonder his head hurt like hell. The mirror on the wall showed a band aid stuck on his forehead. She had wounded him and tended to him at the same time, he chuckled at that thought. What he needed was a strong cup of coffee and aspirin for his aching head. He moved in to his kitchen where he found her humming while she moved around preparing breakfast. She looked rather well settled without a hint of a sleepless night, as if what took place the day before was all in his head.

"Good you are awake." She turned to what she had been doing as if it was an ordinary thing to be preparing a meal in a bachelor's house. "Beth, what are you doing, thought you left" he grumbled as he warily moved towards her. She handed him a glass of water and some aspirin before explaining as if to a child, "I am preparing breakfast, that's what I am doing." Before he could retort further, he resignedly popped the pills into his mouth and gulped them down with water. He moved further away from her onto the other side of the table as he didn't trust himself with her and feared pushing her away by his suddenly awakened male ardor.

She was different from the Beth he met a few months ago. Ever since she gave birth she seemed a lot more mature and one ready to take on everyone at any cost. The dress she was wearing managed to hint at the hips and tiny waist she had, while the damned hairstyle made her look more alluring. God what was happening to him, he wondered as he felt the tell tell signs of arousal and quickly settled down. "Don't you have a child to be taking care of and what will your mom say about all this." She scowled and continued to dish out his breakfast in a plate as he wondered on how domesticated she appeared to be.

"Go home Beth, this is no place for you. What was my mother thinking to leave you here alone" he gruffly spoke before delving into his breakfast. He was starving and wasn't in the mood to talk much. Considering his other state, he would rather concentrate on his food. "Your mother is worried about you Rob. What's going on with you?" She finally settled down across from him with a cup of coffee and concern written all over her face. "Everything is just peachy. Let's leave it at that."

"What about Penelope, she needs her father." He pushed the plate aside having suddenly lost his appetite. So this was about Penny, he tried to bring up the fury he felt for her but nothing instead felt angry with the late mother. "Beth will you please drop this and go home" he ground out. She was pushing him and he wasn't in the mood to play. Instead she stood up and moved to where he sat determination on her face. "Well I will not stop because the last time when I was in hospital it was so easy for you to dish out advice that I wasn't ready to swallow."

He cursed under his breath, remembering her rejection of her son and how quickly he had pointed it out.

"I wasn't aware the pastor now swore" she rebuked as she leaned threateningly over him. "Beth you don't know what you are talking about. My situation is complicated."

She straightened up and settled on the chair next to him. "How so pastor Rob." He grimaced as she addressed him in that manner. He was angry with himself and with God for not warning him about Lisa. All that he was going through could have been avoided if he only knew.

"Penny is not mine, are you happy now" he angrily stated and stood up from the chair. Suddenly he felt the oppressive walls that he always tried to avoid of the house, pressing in on him.

"No it can't be." She answered back as if she might have known Lisa more than he did. "Penny is your child."

He shook his head negatively as she continued, "Have you seen her Rob. Have you looked at her? Those beautiful brown eyes with long lashes, the way she appears to twist her two last fingers unconsciously together and her little pert nose. She is a Parker and definitely your daughter."

He scoffed at that and moved towards the sink where he poured water into the glass. "Believe what you want to believe, Lisa even wrote that she wasn't mine in her diary." He laughed out loud as he thought of the page that had fallen from the bible that made him lose faith in everything.

"So what if she is not yours. She is an innocent in all this. What has she done to deserve your unconcerned attitude towards her? You are her father since you married her mother."

"Beth just drop it" he sighed wearingly as he could hear the sound of her slippers as she moved towards him.

"You know what pastor, you are a hypocrite." He could hear a hard edge to her soft voice as he turned outraged at such an accusation. That pastor word again as she managed to slot it in every time, reminding him of how far he had fallen.

"You can glare at me all you like, but you" she moved close to him and poked his chest, "ruined my life in the form of helping and now when I want to help you act as if I am meddling and want the subject dropped."

He stared at her as her eyes were blazing hot and could have consumed him if he didn't turn away. He hadn't expected to see this side of her as she continued poking him. He finally held her hands firmly and felt a kick on his leg instead. He would have roared out of laughter if two months back, someone had told him Beth would be angry with him and would kick him around. "How have I ruined your life Beth?" he asked a bit confused. Not only was she fighting for a child who wasn't his, she wanted to settle her own score in the process.

"Charles" she spat out.

"Charles?" He really could act out the confused and misunderstood part well, Beth thought as she scowled at him.

"I told you I didn't want to get married but still you went on ahead and planned out the perfect mate for me. Now I have a family waiting for me to do the right thing and accept his proposal."

Robin nearly cursed when he heard that and thought better of it, since she would remind him of a title he didn't want to be associated with. He had totally forgotten about Charles. He heaved a sigh and calmed his nerves before tentatively remarking, "Charles is a good man."

"Wow, are you not the good advisor, one minute you don't want me to get into your business and the next you want to interfere in mine. Can you hear yourself Rob?"

"I was just pointing out..." his voice trailed off as he realized that she had also been pointing out and helping him, just like his mother had tried to, except he had been rude and cruel to her. Lisa was dead, she had betrayed him but was he willing to lose everyone around him so he could feed on the anger he felt over her betrayal. Beth was still glaring angrily at him while he got some light bulbs going on in his mind as he realized what a grizzly he had been for the past two months.

His mother always stated that he usually came out of the deep end swiftly than anyone she knew. "What do you suggest I do pumpy, to solve your problem?" he suddenly smiled taking her off guard. She stared at him suspiciously. Such an instant transformation: from a growling bear to a sweet lamb. "Would you like me to talk to Charles and tell him you are not interested?" She could feel his heart beating as she wasn't aware on when she had splayed her hand over his chest. The Rob she has always known grinned at her, making a mockery of her thoughts in that she had stopped being attracted to him. *His wife just died*, she muttered under her breath as he still curiously stared at her, waiting for the go ahead. "Well," she snatched her hands from his chest as her voice wavered, "I would have told him off except he spoke to my mother and Aunt Rose before he told me. They are so happy and they expect me to accept. This is your fault." She finally slumped on the chair looking dejected as he realized she didn't want to make the same mistake she had before. So if her mother thought Charles was good for her, then she would want to do what's right. He racked his fingers into his hair and dragged out a heavy sigh. "I am sorry Beth. I didn't realize that I had brought this much trouble to you. "

She glared at him, full of disbelief as he chuckled. She sure didn't trust him. He might have been disillusioned for a while, but he was still the same man who believed in love and one day he would get a wife who didn't manipulate him into getting married. "What can I do to resolve this issue, once and for all?" he knelt down near the chair she sat on. "Marry me" she stated simply to his utter shock.

Beth for a second wished for the ground to open up and swallow her alive. Her mother was the culprit for having put such a thought in her mind in the first place. Rob kneeling down and tenderly looking at her only made matters worse. She coughed and downplayed the statement by clearing up her throat and stating, "I mean if you want to help, you can marry me for the children's sake off course. Ryan will have a doting father and Penny a loving mother."

"I thought you didn't want to get married?" Rob frowned and enjoyed making her squirm as she shifted on the kitchen chair. He had thought he was the only one feeling hot and bothered as he realized he was attracted to her but she was also. Thinking back to the night before, he remembered how responsive she had been. He wasn't attracted to her because she looked like Lisa, that was rather a downside since her betrayal still hurt, but Beth was just a breeze of fresh air. He chuckled as he thought back to the day she gave birth. How she was stuck on the doorstep thinking her baby would suddenly fall off if she moved.

She opened her mouth to talk, realizing that Rob wasn't going to say anything as he kept on staring at her, sizing her up. *Mother you have ruined me, her mind kept on screaming.* "I...I..I... gain a father for my son and you gain a mother for your daughter. We both know what betrayal means and I don't want to go the same route. This will be like those arranged marriages, without love, just two people taking care of their children, period."

"Charles has volunteered to be that for you, a father to your son."

She grimaced as he stated that, making it look like Charles was dragged into proposing to her and he didn't have a choice. Gritting out she answered back, "Charles needs someone who will love him and I am no longer capable of that."

He slightly stood up from his kneeling position and leaned near to her face as he watched her lick her lips out of nervousness. "You forgot something in all this Beth." She gulped for air and asked, "What?"

"I might have been betrayed but I haven't given up on love. So what if I do fall in love with someone, what will happen to this arrangement, hmmm?" He rather liked making her uncomfortable and enjoyed seeing her tongue slightly dart out so she could lick her lip. Having tasted her sweetness the day before, he found it rather intoxicating. "Will end it" she finally remarked, as he stared at her in amazement before he kissed her, unable to resist her much longer. He groaned and pulled her closer to him. *What's happening to me,* Beth thought as she clutched at Robs shirt welcoming the assault on her person. "For a woman who wants a loveless marriage you sure are responsive" he commented after they had drawn apart and she hit him on the chest.

"I might not have the capacity to love but I am not dead. I am attracted to you." she simply stated, shocking him again. She was full of surprises. "Liar," he chuckled. Her looking out for him and taking time to talk with him, even fully aware that he might not take her advice, showed she was capable of love. She was just scared, just as he was. He feared that all this could end up being fool's paradise and he had been duped by another woman, again.

"And I am attracted to you" he answered back, hoping to see her blush out of embarrassment. No his Beth was made out of sterner stuff; she chuckled instead and pulled his head back to her, before placing another kiss on his mouth. They might not love each other, but the area pertaining to intimacy was dealt with and he could see that. They heard a car hooting outside and both moved towards the window. "I should go now." Beth said as she realized Bruce was the one making the noise. She glanced at Rob again, still apprehensive over the decision they had both made. "Are you sure about this?"

"I am not, but I expect this will keep the other women at bay." She chuckled at that fact and remarked, "You are so full of it Rob, acting as if you are a gift to women."

"Am I not, while others are knocking at my mother's door, one was brave enough to propose to me. I feel like such a girl right now." She poked at his chest, "You are impossible you know that" she giggled as he held her hands at bay. "And I need to freshen up and talk to my future in-laws." Beth nervously clutched at his hand as it suddenly hit her that she would be getting married. "Beth, I can only leave if you let go of my hand" he stated with a chuckle. "Ooh sorry." she finally dropped her hand but still stood in a daze. "Would you like to join me for a shower" Rob asked with a grin on his face as she gaped in response. "Pastor Rob," she shrieked and watched him resignedly walk away. She finally came out of her daze as Bruce hooted again and rushed for the car, pondering on what she would say to her aunt, her mother would be elated. After all she is the one who had suggested the whole thing.

"BETH WHERE HAVE YOU been" aunt Rose asked when she got into the house. "We were worried sick, well I was worried sick while your mother stated that you were fine at the pastor's house. Are you sure you were at the pastor's house?" Beth chuckled and rushed to hug her aunt. "I am getting married" she whispered and heard her aunt chortle in glee. "We all know that love. Charles is a good man." So her mother didn't inform her aunt that she had also suggested Rob. She settled down at her feet before stating, "Rob not Charles."

"Rob who?"

"Your friend Rob," she laughed as she stared at her gaping mouth. "Now when did that happen?" Aunt Rose asked a bit taken aback. "Rob is moaning his wife; the time is too short for him to contemplate getting married" she stated with an edge to her voice. "The time is long enough; in the ancient times people moaned for a week for their loved ones before they got married again" Ellen explained as she came out of the bedroom with baby Ryan in her arms. "Rob is perfect for Beth. He also has a daughter who needs a mother and Ryan needs a father, Charles doesn't seem to be one who can handle such a responsibility" she concluded and handed Ryan to the mother. Their plan had worked perfectly and she couldn't wait for Tina to hear the news. "I hope you are right in this" Aunt Rose finally said. "I wouldn't want Bethy to be hurt for being married to Rob because he sees a glimpse of his late wife in her."

Beth was leaving the room with Ryan in her arms when her aunt muttered that. She closed the door to her bedroom and placed baby Ryan on the bed before she unzipped her dress at the back. After she had breastfed him and he was sleeping soundly, she moved to her chest of drawers where she had kept the funeral programme. She didn't flip the pages then when it was handed to her. She took out the instant photos taken the day she changed her hairstyle. She had been full of joy then, playing over and over in her head the hug she accidentally received from Rob. Lisa chose that hairstyle for her, she instructed Sharon to cut her hair and style it the way she liked, not how Beth liked. She flipped the pages and came to the photos showing Lisa in different stages of her life. She opened the page with her graduation photo that Sharon had mentioned. Lisa was smiling to the camera, having removed her cap but still dressed in her black graduation gown. Her eyes twinkled as she seemed excited over life like how excited Beth had felt on that day. She stared at both photos. Why hadn't she seen that before? She thought it was all a joke when Rob and Sharon had pointed it out.

Rob was angry with Lisa but he would forgive her. Would he do such a thing as to replace his wife with a look alike because he still loved her? Was she meant to call off everything? Call him and tell him, she couldn't marry him. She stared at herself in the mirror as she saw the reality of it all. She had let her attraction get the best of her, just like on the day that Lisa died. *What have I done,* she wept.

Chapter 7

"WELCOME MRS. PARKER to your new home." Rob chuckled as he swept her off her feet and got into the house. "Put me down," she squirmed in his arms delighting at the same time on how solid he felt. He sauntered into the house with her in his hands and opened the door to the master bedroom before tossing her on the bed as she yelped. There were married within a week of Rob having informed his parents and Beth's family. His mother was delighted and had even changed the décor in the bedroom for Beth's sake. His father as usual had merely nodded and stated that was the best since Penny needed a mother. He also had a weird conversation with his best friend aunt Rose who kept on inserting Lisa into every sentence finally she had seemed satisfied and continued to talk about other things. The downside in everything was the fact that he lost a good friend. Charles had not been impressed at all at the fact that he had moved on so quickly and with the woman he wanted to marry.

It was a small wedding with just a few relatives and friends. Rob had been wonderful during the whole week as they planned out everything. He was overly concerned that she not exert herself too much as she took on an extra child. Right now their children were with Robs parents just across the road. He plopped onto the bed next to her and pulled her to him before tenderly kissing her, as she giggled. "Will you stop goofing around and give me a proper kiss," he chided as she pulled away and dashed for the bathroom. "Beth" he called as he tried to open the door. "I am taking a shower Rob" she called back and giggled. He groaned after having tried to open the door to no avail. She had locked him out, the naughty minx, he thought as he chuckled and lay back on the bed. "Shower is free," she shouted when she came out of the bath and smirked. He rose from the bed and commented, "For a person about to receive her goodies, you sure look like one visiting the North Pole." She giggled and waved her hand dismissively as his eyes racked over her body and he whistled. She was dressed like an Eskimo.

"The weather is a bit nippy, didn't you notice that," she stated rolling her eyes as if she wasn't acting out of the ordinary. "Are you sure everything is fine pumpy," Rob asked as she pushed him towards the bath. "Peachy perfect. Come down for supper when you are done, I am starving" She stated before she left the room. He raised his brow wondering on what was happening. He had noticed a bit of reservations ever since he visited her mother and aunt but thought nothing about it. *What are you up to Beth,* he thought as he got into the bathroom.

ROBIN GOT INTO THE kitchen and settled down on the chair as Beth moved around, reminding him of how he had desired her a week ago when he saw her in his kitchen. It suddenly appeared as if they had been married for a long time as she was more comfortable in his kitchen, while he still felt like a stranger in his own home. "Ta da" she produced the food with flourish, what he had eaten then. Bacon, scrambled eggs and coffee. "Beth, is that our supper," he asked with a chuckle as she settled down. He wasn't hungry at all after the wedding meal he had at his parents place. "Well pastor Rob, before this goes further," she stated eliciting a scoff from him. "I don't know how to cook."

He stared at her disbelief evident on his expression as he asked. "What about the meals you used to say you are preparing?" he asked as she giggled nervously, "My mom put me on lunch duty for that. If you want a mean sandwich, I can make it for you." He burst out laughing as his picture of a domesticated Beth faded away. "Lisa was actually a very good cook. Surprised that didn't rub onto you," he chortled and realized his mistake after. "I am not Lisa in case you didn't notice"

"Honey I didn't mean you are?" This was getting out of hand so suddenly. "So why did you have to bring her up and point out how good she was in the kitchen."

"Geez love" he sighed and moved towards her, "I didn't mean it that way and you know it. What is going on Beth? You have been acting this way throughout the week. Don't you think you should have voiced out your concerns before we tied the knot?"

"Wow I didn't see that coming," she glowered back at him as he was surprised by her anger. "What are you trying to say Rob that I trapped you and now I am acting out?"

He had been about to pull her into his arms but waved them in defeat instead and walked away. This was ridiculous as she was totally putting words in his mouth.

"I think its best we stuck to why we got married. The children" she mumbled as he stared at her in horror. Wow, she truly was revealing her fangs before their marriage had a chance. Lisa had been more subtle than that. "You know what Beth, fine." He stood up from the chair he had returned to and left the house, banging the door after him. Women, he failed to understand them.

"DIDN'T EXPECT TO SEE you here Rob? Thought you would be enjoying the pretty lady you married" Charles commented as he settled down next to him in the private lounge. He gulped down his scotch before paying and stood up. He had been nursing his drink for a while as he played out the scene that had taken place in his house. Now Charles was glaring at him, looking for a fight also which he had tried to avoid with his wife. Charles hadn't taken the whole thing lightly when he explained that he would be marrying Beth. He had rather become insulting and Rob walked away. He didn't mention it to Beth not wanting her to get worried. He had set them up and he understood his friend's feelings over the whole situation. "Where are you going Pst Rob? Let's have a drink together" he chuckled and continued, "and talk about the pretty thing you married. She is a fast one that one." He grinned as Rob growled, "that's my wife you are talking about, if you knew what's good for you, you would mind what you say"

"What will you do about it? I never thought you would go for the same kind of woman like Lisa, who played you throughout and you didn't realize that" his diatribe was cut short as he found himself sprawled on the floor while his jaw ached and Rob walked out of the door. He tasted blood in his mouth before he followed his once best friend and lunged at him as they toppled outside onto the ground.

BETH WAS FEELING GUILTY over how she had suddenly lashed out on Rob. He was indeed right; she should have voiced out her concerns before and not have bottled them up like she did. Throughout the week she had the chance to do so, but she fooled herself into thinking everything would work out. Rob saw her and not Lisa. How could he have suddenly moved on so fast as if the two months he had been grumpy and hurting hadn't taken place? Was it that she was trying to cling to the ghost, while it was a possibility that he really had gotten over Lisa's betrayal. She sighed out loudly thinking on how she could make it up to him and apologize for blowing things out of proportion. She was feeling hot in the clothes and she was scared too. A lot of things were going on in her mind as she thought of her one time with Jeffrey in the car. He later called her frigid. *No Jeffrey I will not let you take away my happiness. Lisa is dead and so are you, you are under that brand,* she muttered as she shed off her clothes. She took out a filmy nightie she had received from her aunt and wore it while she stared at herself in the mirror.

Rob might not love her but they could certainly have roaring sex together, find comfort in each other, than hold onto ghosts that had no place in their new life. She ruffled up her hair to look like one coming from bed and smiled. If Rob wasn't going to pant after her after this, he had to be a saint indeed, she thought as she heard the sound of the door being shut. *Good he is back*, she thought as she moved towards the living room where she found him leaning over the fireplace with an iron poker in his hand. "Rob" she whispered as he answered gruffly, "Go to bed love, I will see you tomorrow." He didn't turn to look at her and he hadn't switched on the overhead lamp. The light in the room was coming from the fireplace. She cleared up her throat and moved towards him. "I just wanted to apologize for the way I acted today."

"Its fine Beth, just go to bed."

Why was he insisting that she leave, she drew closer sniffing the air, he had been drinking. Reaching out to the switch on the wall, she angrily flipped it on and stared with horror as she could see clearly that he had been in a brawl. There was a cut on his forehead, while his eye had reddened up. "What happened," she shouted as she drew closer to him and touched the cut on the forehead that had already dried blood on the sides. He chuckled at seeing how concerned she was as she pulled him to the couch and made him sit on it, before she left for the bathroom where the first aid kit was kept. Rob suddenly missed her jerseys and tracksuit as she leaned in to look closely on the wound. Apart from battling with the pain of losing a friend and on his eye, he now had to fight the urge to pull her into his arms and kiss her senselessly.

"Had a run in with Charles," he drawled and flinched as she dabbed on the wound. Did the woman realize what a temptation she was? He could feel her breath on the wound as she puffed out some warm air on it before dressing it and placing a band aid over it. "Charles did this to you?" she asked incredulous at the fact. He flinched as she pressed harder on his forehead, "and to think you wanted to marry me off to such a violent man."

The woman sure knew how to fizzle out his passion by just being cruel. "Beth," he ground out as she tenderly tended to the spot she had wounded. "I hope you returned a few blows also on him. What were you fighting about by the way?"

"You, I took away the love of his life" he stated as she scowled, "fighting over a woman, tsk tsk, am disappointed in you Pastor Rob." There was a slight pause as he gulped down some air over how closely she was leaning as she tended to him.

"Beth, I am sorry if I made you uncomfortable by mentioning Lisa. I wasn't comparing you with her in any way. If you prefer that I don't say her name in your presence, I will not." At least if they stuck to the neutral topic, his mind would not wander like what it was doing, he reasoned.

"Don't be silly" she stated brightly, "She was your wife and the love of your life, I wouldn't expect you to forget about her. I am the one who should be sorry. Well I thought..." her voice faltered as she finally settled down next to him on the couch and guiltily looked away from him. "What did you think?"

"I thought you married me because I look like her."

"Who the hell gave you such a harebrained idea," he spoke softly and not at all angry as she would have expected. When she looked up to his roughed up face she almost laughed. She was seeing at first hand the rumors that had circulated that he got involved in brawls also. So much for the preaching he might have given people pertaining to giving the other cheek also. She could see his Adams apple bobble up and down as he swallowed. So her nightie was a distraction after all, just as she had intended. Having stated that it was all for the kids, she knew he would not touch her unless she gave him a hint. "Shall we go to bed," she asked and stood up from the couch before she placed the first aid box on the coffee table. "Rob"

"Yes, bed. We can" he trailed behind her as she could feel his eyes on her back. She was attracted to him, even when he looked the worse for wear. She slid into the bedcovers and waited as he went to the bathroom. She hoped he took the hint as she didn't know what else to do. Especially after she had stupidly voiced out that their relationship was strictly for the children's sake. She wished she could take it all back. He came back as she watched him move to the wardrobe and take out a blanket which he spread on their carpeted floor. Seriously, he was making it harder than she had anticipated. She suddenly had an image of her begging on her knees that he made love to her.

"You take the bed and I will sleep on the floor" he stated as if she hadn't seen what he was doing. "The bed is big enough," she retorted as he chuckled and reluctantly slid under the covers. "Good night" he stated before he turned the other side and switched off his side lamp. She huffed and he could hear the irritation in her voice as she mumbled "good night."

She wasn't strong then to resist her attraction to him after all, he thought. That was why she fought with him, so she would be angry and went to bed miffed, rather than face the act. He chuckled. "Why are you laughing?"

"Well for a person who settled for a chaste marriage, you are acting all irritated and grumpy like a sex starved woman." He was turning to face her when he got hit by a pillow in his face. "Ouch, head and eye injury remember." She had already shifted when he yelped and her hand was already on his forehead as she puffed out breaths of warm air over his eye. "So sorry I hurt you" she whispered. "Let me kiss and make it better." He chuckled as she did just that. "This is for blowing things out of proportion" she placed a kiss on the eye. "This is for thinking the worst about you" she placed it on the nose, "this is for your fight with Charles" she placed it on the cheek, "and lastly this is for my stupid stupiiiid idea of a chaste marriage" she placed the kiss on the lips. She sighed as he didn't respond the way she anticipated and turned over to sleep. He was laughing, good for him, she thought as he chortled out of glee and turned her back to face him. "Come here you. Do you think I can resist a scantily clad woman like you" he grinned before kissing her slowly and tenderly, making her want to scream. "So is intimacy now back on the table?" he asked as she giggled and he went on to kiss and make her feel cherished and loved as they finally consummated their marriage.

Chapter 8

BETH STRETCHED OUT her body in bed and sighed out of contentment. She was still groggy with sleep, yet she had to get up. It had been a month after her prompt wedding and she was rather enjoying her new family life. Rob had taken some leave days from work so he could help her out with the children as they transitioned to a rather noisy household. She reached out to the other side of the bed and realized Rob wasn't on her side. She wondered where he had gone to as he came through the door with a tray with food. "Morning Mrs. Parker," he greeted with a smile and placed the tray on the side chest. "How do you take your tea?" She giggled as she watched him attend to her needs. "What are you plans for today?" she asked as they had their breakfast in bed. "Thought we were sleeping in" He winked at her as she blushed. Finally, he loved seeing her blush than be stern and address him as pastor when he did or said something naughty. It was after they were done eating and lay in bed when Beth asked, "Is they any chance that you will go back into ministry." He shook his head negatively, "I don't think I will"

"Why not, why did you leave anyway, Lisa's betrayal wouldn't have made you give up on God, would it." He grinned at the fact that she didn't pretend or mince around, but rather asked not caring if he would be offended or not. He wasn't. "Let's say I realized I wasn't ready for it. It was so easy to give out advice, but when I got my own test, I failed dismally and I didn't want to be a hypocrite, what you claimed I was by the way." She giggled at that, "maybe in future, when I am older and wiser." She rolled her eyes at that as his grin widened. "For now I will concentrate on my family" he lightly tapped her cute nose, "and on the mechanic workshop. What about you."

"What about me?" She shifted and lay on her tummy with one hand placed below her cheek as she stared at him. "Your mom mentioned you were one of the lead singers in your church choir"

"I don't know if I will join the choir again" she muttered. He searched out a song that would be in the universal hymn book and sang out a verse as her eyes widened. Ooh boy he could sing, he motioned with his hand for her to sing the next verse and sat up at the first note. She giggled when she was done as he kept on gawking at her. He sang the chorus and she joined in. He leapt off the bed afterwards as he stated, "well, well Mrs. Parker, I think we should make an album"

She was giggling at his antics as he continued, "I am going to be rich, riiich"

"Ha, ha stop goofing around," she chided good humoredly. He knelt near the bed before grasping at her hands. "Since you are not yet sure pertaining to joining a choir, why don't you start with the Sunday school children?" She suddenly had an idea when he mentioned that, "On one condition" she smirked as he looked at her suspiciously. Did he just fall into one of her traps? "You come back to church." He could literally hear money changing hands as he had overhead his mother bet with his dad that Beth would have him back in church in no time. He growled and finally gave in, "you drive a hard bargain pumpy. I will come back, can we shake on it."

She giggled as he vigorously shook her hand. "By the way do you happen to be one of the women who love the suits and the wide breamed hats? Maybe that's the only reason you want me to come back. So you are ushered in with an entourage, looking all pretty and made up"

Beth burst into fits of laughter as once upon a time she had wished for that kind of a life. "No I am not"

"Are you sure, he asked and covered her forehead with his hand as he imagined a hat in its place. "You would look charming" he commented before kissing her.

ON SUNDAY AS AGREED the whole family attended the service. A three month old Penny was in Beth's arms dressed up in a lacy pink dress and bonnet, while Rob had the son in his arms dressed in a matching black suit like him. At six months, Ryan seemed big and with his dark hair could have been mistaken for Rob's biological son.

The small family settled on the pews reserved for the Parker family. Tina was elated when she saw her son and kept on grinning at him. Just as she had thought, Beth was indeed good for her son and she had made him come back to the world of the living. Rob smiled more, he visited their family home with his wife frequently and he seemed to be back to his old self. Unknown to them, as they enjoyed the service a person seated at the far corner of the church watched them and became even more infuriated as Beth and Rob for a second gazed at each other, smiling and oblivious to the world. He had had enough. He got up from his seat and left the church. It was unfair that Rob got everything he ever wanted. First it was Lisa and now he was having a great time with his small family. No, that was his daughter and he was going to make sure he got her just to spite his once best friend. He could just imagine the anguish on Robin's face when he told him that he was the father and not him. The hurt he will feel. For a man who had claimed to love Lisa, he surely didn't take much time to moan about her. He seemed to have forgotten so quickly. Just after three months he had married and he was proudly showing the whole world that he was in love with the new woman.

Taking away the daughter would be a good thing. Lisa deserved much better than just being a flitting memory as everyone who claimed to have loved her moved on with their lives. Beth had never stared at him the way she did Rob. Did the two have an affair that Lisa found out about and that's why she was dead? She had been healthy and happy, full of life and in no way at deaths door. *They killed her and now are blatantly flaunting their love for each other. I will make them pay, they will all pay for taking my precious Lisa away from me,* Charles thought as he strode away from the church premises with a light back in his steps.

Chapter 9

"HAPPY BIRTHDAY SWEETIE" Rob whispered as he stared at her rouse from her sleep. He had been staring at her beautiful face while she slept and thinking of the spitfire she could be when angry. There was never a dull day with her. "How did you know," she asked after receiving a tender kiss from her husband. "Your mother," before he could continue the baby started crying and another followed as they resignedly went back to their normal routine. She rose from the bed and wore a purple silk bathrobe over her nighty before she followed Rob who was cooing at Penny screaming her lungs out. She plucked Ryan from his crib and changed his wet clothes before exchanging with Rob. She chuckled at how well there seemed to work together and she wasn't aware when Rob started holding Penny. But there he was, doing that. It must have been unconsciously, when she was tending to Ryan's needs when he held her. "Sweetie, don't cry" she cooed to her daughter and chuckled, "the grizzly bear will not hurt you"

Rob grumbled as she remarked, "did you look at yourself in the mirror, and you expect poor Penny to not cry out at seeing you. What's with the caveman look?"

"Told you I am trying out a new look, so I get selected by the Sunday school teacher to act as Joseph in the Christmas play."

She giggled at that as he whispered to Ryan who gurgled cutely. "Let's leave these two girls, we are not needed here" before sauntering off from the nursery. She settled on the rocking chair, covering Penny warmly before breastfeeding her. The doctor had given a go ahead for her to breastfeed Penny along with Ryan. She had learnt to look at them as twins despite the three months difference. Her mother had been right in suggesting she got married to Rob after all. Rob was indeed a good father to Ryan as she looked at Penny also as her own. Penny was indeed hers, how could she not be when her tiny mouth tugged at her nipple and an overwhelming love flowed from mother to daughter. "Good girl" she whispered as she placed her over her shoulder so she could burp. She chuckled when she heard the sound and placed her back in her crib. "Mommies little angel," she whispered as she watched Penny's little feet splay around and she caught hold of the huge plastic toy keys she handed to her. "That's not food," she chuckled at her cute little mouth sucking at the plastic. "Are you done?" Rob had been watching his beautiful wife and child for some time before making his presence known. "Ryan needs a diaper change." Beth scoffed as Rob's grin widened. He surely knew how to take advantage of her. He was quick to hand over the kids when they did a number two, but would easily change them if it was just a wet nappy. So she had become the poopy woman. "Don't get up from the chair, I will change him."

"You change him?" she incredulously blurted out. "You are the birthday girl, remember," he smirked before he moved to the little counter where he laid Ryan and got busy changing his diaper.

"So what do you want for your birthday" he asked as he pinned Ryan's diaper and threw the soiled one in a bin at the corner of the counter. "Just being with you and the kids is perfect."

"Well I don't think that will happen. Both our mothers were acting as if they have something big planned out." Penny was still concentrating on the keys so she rushed to her husband and grabbed his arm. "What do you think it is?" He shrugged off her hand and took Ryan to his crib that was next to Penny and laughed as she joyously stated what she hoped for. "They will be a carriage and I will be dressed like Ella, a princess," she sighed. "You should dress like a knight, I prefer a costume party, and so you fence around with your sword."

He burst out laughing at her antics. "What, it's my last year of being a teen after all. Nineteen is not a joke."

"Wow I hadn't realized I robbed the cradle," he laughed as she scowled. "How is it any different from you wanting to be Joseph in a children's play."

"For starters Joseph is real and blood coursed through his veins. And why not use me, Sunday school teacher, I have the beard, than take a child whose face is smooth and paste on a funny looking beard. Ella on the other hand is fiction, that's the difference my love."

"Ooh you, such a party pooper," she stated as he pulled her into his arms. "I know you like the beard, it makes me look distinguished" he stated as he brushed it over her sensitive neck before kissing her.

HER DAY WAS NOTHING but ordinary as the hours passed by. Her phone started ringing, startling her from her unfulfilled daydream costume party. It was her mother, since Rob had hinted they had planned something for her, she hoped this was it. "Sweet heart, I want to wish you a happy birthday," her mother spoke in her soft voice from the other end of the line. "Thank you mom" she replied as her mother promised she would bring her gift over to her house. "Rob informed me that you had rather spend it with your small family so didn't want to interrupt and cause havoc to your plans," she stated with a chuckle as Beth gritted her teeth. That's why the big thing that Rob had mentioned hadn't come to fruition. "That's Rob, my helpful and considerate husband." Her mother laughed at that as she could sense the irritation in her voice. "I hope you are not angry with Rob darling."

"I am not."

"Ok see you soon when I bring the gift." Beth stared at the phone with disbelief. It rang again and she accepted the birthday wishes. Her friends and family started calling as if they were lined up at a public phone booth doing so. The minute she hung up, another call would come through. Finally when she was done with the calls she moved to her living room expecting to find her helpful husband except he wasn't there. The library, the kid's nursery. She bit at her lip wondering where he could be. Her phone rang again as she answered it. "Happy birthday Beth. Can you please come over and collect some of Penny's stuff that was left this side" Tina said before hanging up. That was odd she thought as Beth had stayed for a month with Rob without the stuff being mentioned. She shrugged her shoulders and walked out of the house across the street to her in-laws. She knocked on the door and got in.

There was no one. Where had everyone gone to? She moved to the library as her father in law tended to be in it, writing out sermons or reading the wide range of books they had. When she opened the door, her heart almost stopped beating as people jumped out screaming surprise!! At the top of their lungs. Her mother came in from among the crowd. "Happy birthday darling she remarked as Beth chuckled marveling at her Marilyn Monroe look. Everyone was dressed in costumes, when did they plan that out and where was her husband. "Aunt Courtney" she screamed as the woman approached her dressed as Maleficent. "Hello ducky, happy birthday dear." Her father in law hugged her and the rest of the family wishing her a happy birthday while her husband was nowhere to be found. "Where is Rob?" she whispered to her mother in law as they settled for dinner."

"He must be with the kids. He is such a devoted father isn't he" Tina winked at her and resumed with her meal. What was going on with Rob, she wondered. After dinner the cake was cut as they sang a birthday song for her, still Rob was nowhere to be found. "Time for you to change dear" her mother in law stated as she led her to the guest room where she found a costume laid out on the bed for her. How did you manage all this she screamed while her mother in law simply stated, "your devoted husband?"

The cheek of a man, he knew all the time he had planned out the perfect birthday for her. Dressing up in the off white boob tube ball gown that had intricately woven beads on the waist and a flared skirt. She giggled when her mother in law placed a golden tiara over her head as her fairy tale birthday theme came true. She was shocked when they walked down the corridor since she hadn't looked at her in-laws house properly, to be ushered into a ballroom, elegantly decorated and the guests waiting for her. They gasped and sighed, opening a path in the middle and there at the end stood her dashing husband looking more like an aristocrat with his dark hair parted on the side. He grinned, revealing the dimple on his clean shaven cheek. She erased the knight image in her mind; never would she want him to do a sword play as she preferred his current look. She stared at his attire that snugly wrapped around his body like a second skin as he moved towards her and slightly bowed. She giggled before he ask, "May I have this dance." Music was playing in the back grounds, she curtsied feeling silly and blushing to her roots as she was taken into his arms and he twirled her around the room. The rest of her family members and friends joined in. Her mom winked at her as she danced with Mr. Wilkinson. "Did I do anything to displease you my princess," Rob whispered into her ear managing to send some tingling sensations over her body. She chuckled at how he was addressing her, enjoying acting out her fantasy. "No, this is perfect. Am speechless."

"That's a first," he grumbled and got his foot trod on in return for saying that. Her father in law, cut into their dance and smirked as his son scowled and moved away. "Thank you for this," she whispered. He smiled, "No thank you for bringing back our son to us."

"Rob would have come around eventually," she scoffed as her father in law burst out laughing. "Maybe. Look at him now, being all jealous and protective." They looked to where he stood and just like her father in law had mentioned, he was standing astride, disapprovingly looking their way as if they weren't any women to dance with. "Let's make him jealous even further," her father in law winked as he motioned for Joey who happened to be a deacon in his church and also Rob's friend. "Looking beautiful as always Beth," he whispered as they danced. "Thank you." She enjoyed his company as they chatted oblivious to an irritated husband.

Finally Rob gave up the fight of watching his wife dance with other men and interrupted them. She looked so beautiful and carefree. Her eyes twinkled as she knew she had been goading him on. "I think it's time to make our exit," he whispered as he took her hand and moved to his parents, her mother, grandaunt and the rest, making their farewells. The children would remain with his parents. She thought they would be going to their house but was shocked to see what awaited her outside. "Bethy you got your birthday dream after all" her mom chuckled as they came outside with the rest of the small party to see them off. A white carriage being drawn by a black horse was at standstill. "Shall we" Rob asked as the other guests clapped hands and whistled. She settled on the seat in the carriage as he followed suit before they rode off. "How did you manage all this?"

"Surprised you have been in this small town for a while but you haven't realized that the residents love costume parties."

"Oh you", she pinched his arms as the horse trotted on the empty street. "Didn't you see the billboard as you came into this town?"

"What billboard?"

"Welcome to Graceland where your fairytale dreams are fulfilled." She chuckled remembering she had scoffed at it then as she was feeling dejected from being rejected by Jeffrey. "Thank you for this" she whispered and lay back on his shoulder as the carriage moved along the well-lit street. Finally it came to a standstill at the park and the carriage driver got off, nodded to them before leaving them to their privacy.

"I have a gift for you." Rob took out the wrapped out box from below the seat and handed it over to her.

"What is it" she excitedly enquired shaking the box. "Just open it love." She quickly unwrapped it and stared at the box wondering what it held. Looking at the size she thought a diary of some sort. She opened it as her breath caught when she realized it was a laminated birth certificate of Ryan Parker and the father's name had been entered as Robin Parker.

"You shouldn't have" she whispered as tears fell from her eyes. "You, Ryan and Penny are my life. Ryan might not be my biological child but I have become his legal father." She threw her arms around him overwhelmed by his care. "You don't know what this means to me," she sniffled. Rob would never realize the precious gift he had given to her son. The blank space on her birth certificate always used to make her wonder if she was unwanted. She always felt her identity as incomplete as her faceless father never made the effort to look for her. No matter how her mom put it, she was incomplete just as her birth certificate was. Ryan would not have to experience that.

"Hush now my love; this is not the time to cry. It's your birthday, rejoice." He handed a handkerchief for her to wipe the tears away. "Another gift to my lovely wife," this time he produced a small long box. She opened it and found a necklace intricately woven nestled in it. She opened the heart shaped locket and a pic of her and Rob was on one side while a pic of the children was on the other. "This is beautiful, thank you" she whispered and tenderly kissed him. "I love you," she whispered and was shocked as she realized that she really did love him. Rob held her firmly tilting her face so she wouldn't look away. "And I love you" he said before kissing her. They hugged and she laid her head on his chest, content with how life had worked out for good after all. She remembered the prayer she once made and realized that indeed God had been faithful and Ryan now had a steady home. She also got a man who loved her.

Chapter 10

"I DON'T KNOW MOTHER in law, I will talk to him" Beth finally stated and took a sip of the tea. Tina sighed as she looked relieved at the outcome. "I know going back there might bring bad memories, Rob can always attend alone." Beth smiled at how thoughtful her mother in law was. "I will be fine. Its Rob am more worried about. Don't you think you are just being too quick in the whole matter?" Tina scoffed as she intended her son to come around fast and return to ministry. "He did mention that he would return in future."

"I will be no more by then my dear," Tina answered eliciting a chuckle from Beth. "How are the Christmas carols coming along?" Beth gushed as she explained the progress that the children had made as they had started practicing for the Christmas festival special. Rob had seized bothering her over acting as Joseph after she stated that the Easter drama would be acted out by the youths. He had settled for Peter yet she thought he would make a great depiction of Jesus. After chatting with her mother in law, she left for her house. She had hired a nanny to take care of the kids hence she found time to also include new things into her life. She was taking cooking lessons and Rob had tasted some of her charred dishes and advised she stuck to sandwiches. As it turned out Lisa actually learnt homemaking from courses offered at church and to think Beth had always thought her to be the epitome of womanhood. Beth still couldn't believe that Lisa could have been that heartless as to the point of trapping Rob. She felt that they were some missing links as the Lisa she knew loved her husband even when she had been surly with him.

She couldn't guess for sure if what Rob said was what he read out since he tore and burnt the paper. Despite the hurt he might have felt, Rob was a great husband to her and she was grateful that he loved her. "Hey honey thought you were still at work." Beth remarked as she got into the house and found Rob in the living room with a newspaper in hand. "Just came in a while ago." He pulled her into his lap before noisily kissing her. She giggled and finally sat on the couch. "What about you, are you done with the practice?"

"Yes" she nodded and smirked wondering on how to brooch the subject. Rob continued with his paper and finally put it aside after taking note that she was staring at him. "Spill it,"

She nervously giggled before stating, "No one wants to rush you into anything. You can always say no." Already he knew what was coming and let her continue, smothering a laugh as she shifted around. His mother's advocate was now at work. These two could be the death of him. "As you know your father has a lot on his plate."

"My father has the help of a lot of elders and deacons." Beth fluttered her arms, having her sails knocked off. She stood up and settled back on her husband's lap before coyly staring at him with half closed eyes. Now the seduction technique. He was rather enjoying himself as she stroked his chest and purred. "Well even the deacons have an overload of work." She looked up and noticed the mischievous smirk on his face and scowled. "You already know what I was about to say?"

"Yes, do tell my mom that her advocate failed dismally." She huffed and stood up but was pulled back into his arms. "Its fine love, we will go" he grinned. "Dad spoke to me about that. I hope you don't mind that I agreed."

"Not at all." she shyly smiled as he raised a brow, "I don't think it's a good idea, seeing how you are already anticipating something naughty.

Who do you intend to meet dear wife? A rendezvous of some sort." She lightly hit him on the chest, "Don't be silly, just some few friends that my husband should meet." He grinned; she was that kind of woman, who loved announcing she was the pastor's wife. He guessed that she had already called her friends and informed them she would be with them at the conference. Her mother had initially filled him in with the events that happened to her at her former town. He loved how she appeared to have risen above that and she seemed not to be having any grudges towards anyone. She had still kept in touch with her friends including Joan, Jeffrey's sister.

He knew they were best friends though it had taken some time for her to tell him the name of the father's child. Since her mother had hinted that none of the women believed her, he understood why she was hesitant over his name. He knew Jeffrey since they had attended the same Bible College. He rather delighted in the pomp and display while he flaunted the prophetic gift as if he was the only one who heard from God. Agreeing on the trip would be good for Beth, she could finally get the closure she needed, that's why he agreed when his father asked him to go in his stead. "Are you done with packing then?" She stared at him outraged at the assumption before answering, "They are just a few things I still need to pack," and rushed towards their bedroom. He laughed and returned to his paper shaking his head. Boy was he in trouble.

"SO WHAT NEXT?" BETH watched her husband unloosen his tie. They were back in their hotel room after having attended the morning service. He smirked as she removed her wide breamed black hat. "I know what you are thinking Pastor Parker, this is all on your mom, she chose the wardrobe."

"Continue telling yourself that," he grinned and settled on the couch. "I am on in the evening so I was wondering if you will help me out." He sheepishly looked her way as she slumped onto the bed. "What do you want me to do?"

Standing up, he walked towards her and settled on the bed before explaining to her what needed to be done. She knew that congregants could be difficult at times and they needed an atmosphere to encourage them to worship the Lord. Rob already had a few selections of songs she would have to sing. "You are the best." He whispered after he was done as she blushed at the complement. The short reprieve from church gave him the time to write out a few notes on what he would preach; hence he left her to rest.

"BETH" HILLARY AND JOAN shrieked as she came out of the huge building. The ministers and their wives were the first ones to leave the church, therefore since Hillary and Joan where on the ushering team, they got out with them. Beth excitedly rushed to them and hugged her two girlfriends. "How did you find the service today" she asked and winked at them as they giggled. "Powerful" Joan remarked and widened her eyes when she saw the pastor coming their way. The night was cool with a slight breeze while they stood on the well-lit premises of the hall where they held the conference. Right across the street was the hotel where the ministers and their wives were staying for the three days while they had the conference. He smiled and managed to make the two ladies blush. "Ladies, this is my husband, Pastor Robin Parker. Rob, these are my best friends, Hillary and Joan." The two ladies shook his hand as he tried very hard to keep a straight face. By the way they were staring at him; he knew they were clergy crazy. He excused himself from the ladies so they could talk freely and joined the rest of the ministers going to the private room booked out for them for relaxation before they retired for the night. "Well, well, you are so secretive girl" Joan remarked after as Beth scowled at her good humoredly. "I am not" she denied, "I told you that I was getting married, it was a prompt wedding and I even invited you. You said you had exams," she pointed at Hills, "and you didn't have leave days from work." Hillary flagged her hand, "I didn't say anything. You know I would have attended the ceremony if it weren't for school"

"Yes love." Joan looked at her conspiratorially, considering the fact that she was the pastors daughter, Joan tended to be crazy over man of the cloth. Beth remembered a time when she had remarked as they grew older that she will only get married to someone like her dad. She already knew what she would ask before she did. "By the way Beth, are there any more handsome single young pastors in G land. You forgot to mention that Rob was young. Thought your ma had given you off to a middle aged man. He does not look at all the widower you portrayed." Beth giggled, "Ha ha, Rob is the only one." She laughed out loud after noticing their shocked expressions. "Why don't you visit and you will find out."

"What I am most interested in knowing is this," Hillary enjoined the conversation, "How does it feel to be married to a pastor" Beth was already rolling her eyes at the antics of her friends. "Rob is not a pastor, he was just helping out his father by coming out for this conversion."

"You could have fooled us," Joan muttered under her breath as she pointed out, "with the way you were going around the pulpit, the gospel duo and the preaching. That's a minister even if he denies it. I even had goose bumps as he preached on and could swear I heard angels singing along when you both sang."

"Stop it Joan" Hillary and Beth managed to say in unison as they laughed. "Enough about me. So what has been happening, in this small community of yours." They moved towards the benches situated outside the church and settled there. Her friends filled her in on the things taking place. "By the way, they have been rumors that some girls came forward and complained that Jeffrey touched them inappropriately on different occasions. So an investigation is being made." Hilary stated on a sober note. "Are you serious? What a pity." Joan glared at her and Beth had to ask, "What."

"Well just didn't expect you to react in this manner, considering what he did to you. Thought you would say, he got what he deserved."

"Stop being silly Jo, he happens to be your brother also, don't you pity him for taking the wrong path. I guess your mom tried to shut the whole story up." Jo nodded. Beth had thought that if she told Jo the truth about her relationship with her brother she would despise her, but she never did. Instead she was a pillar of strength unto her and was rather bothered on the callous manner in which her brother and mother acted.

"How is your dad doing?"

"You know the minister," she chuckled, "he merely said one reaps what they sow. Put the harshest of penalties in place. Jeff will no longer hold a post until further notice that is if his name is cleared of all the charges."

"Tsk, tsk. How are the girls coping and who are there?" Hills shrugged her shoulders, "We don't know. It has been kind of hush hush as they stated that it might be hard for any others to come forward considering Jeff does have a bit of blind followers. So the disclosure of their names might do them more harm than good. Already they are some ladies who have been posting nasty comments online stating to touch not the anointed servant of God." They all sighed and moved on to the next topic, catching up on the time there had been apart. Beth was grateful for getting the opportunity to see them again. "It's been nice seeing you girls," Beth remarked as she hugged them and kissed them on each cheek. "Tell you what, you line up the bachelors and will visit over the Christmas holiday," Jo suggested. "Deal. I have to go, tired and need extra sleep which I will not get when am back home with those two noisy kids around." Her friends giggled at that sentiment. "Still can't believe our Bethy girl is a mother of two." Hillary commented and received a swat on the arm. "Will you be joining the ministers' wives in the private lounge? Wish I could be a fly on their wall right now." Jo sighed. "And have to deal with your mother's glares, nope, am going straight to bed. Rob will have to get through this storm alone." They had arrived at the entrance of the hotel. She hugged them for the last time before she entered it. Knowing her friends, they would stand at the door for an hour chatting, hence she had to leave fast before temptation sank in. she was relieved to find Rob not yet back, as she needed to sleep early and not have him disturb her wanting her attention.

She took a quick shower and dressed in her nightie before sliding into the cool sheets. She must have dozed off because the next moment, she woke up hearing a knock on the door. *Must be Rob and he forgot his key card;* she thought as she rushed to the door and opened the door with a disapproving expression pasted on her face. She was shocked when she realized her blunder and tried to close the door. He pushed the door effortlessly and smirked, "hi princess, it's been long."

Having seen Rob sauced before she sniffed the air and knew he was drunk. Did ministers have to resort to drinking when life took a nose dive? Rob had promised he would never drink and had stood by that promise.

"Jeff what are you looking for here," she angrily asked as she suddenly tried to hide her body with her arms. He perused over her body and the glance made her feel that she would faint on the spot. The rumors were true after all, he was a menace. "Get out, my husband will be here any moment." He sneered as he drew closer and she edged away from him. "Princess, this will not take time and it will be our little secret. For the sake of the love we both shared for each other. We have that bond remember. The child and also the reality that I was your first."

Beth frantically searched for something she could use as a weapon to defend herself from him. She was so relieved when she heard the click on the door as Rob opened it. "Thank God you are back," she yelled as she rushed to him. Jeffrey stood, unwavering as if he wasn't doing anything wrong, while Beth clutched at her husband. "Pastor Robin," he finally spoke before he looked and winked at Beth. "Another time princess," he continued before moving out of the room and closing the door behind him.

"I am so glad to see you," Beth nervously remarked as she shifted and stood in front of Rob. He wasn't looking at her and she sensed he was angry but wondered why he would be. She hadn't done anything wrong. "Next time, please meet up with your ex somewhere else rather than our room," he blandly stated to her utter shock. "What are you talking about?"

"Make your rendezvous somewhere else, and as a reminder, we might be married because of the children but I expect you to be faithful." She flinched at the implication of what he meant and stared at him, only to be met by brown eyes that had suddenly gone cold.

"No Rob, you can't think I invited him to our room," she retorted back, stricken at the fact that he might think that about her. "Hmmmm," he looked over her body with his eyes coming to the filmy nighty she was wearing. She heaved a sigh as she wasn't ready to invite a ghost of a person who made him insecure and fight with him at the same time. "You know what. Think what you want. I am tired and going to bed." She curtly said before sliding back into bed and shutting her eyes. Rob stood in the middle of the room, not believing she had just done that. She had seemed relieved when he got into the room, yet he couldn't stop himself from thinking the worst. Lisa lied and Beth was capable of that as well. Especially with the history she shared with Jeff. He gritted his teeth angrily before moving to the other side of the bed, where he chucked off his clothes and slid into it. Beth was softly snoring away as if nothing had happened. Grunting, he turned to the other side and fitfully fell asleep.

Chapter 11

BETH HEAVED OUT A SIGH, as she listened to the Minister preaching for the morning service. Rob had been glaring at her ever since she woke up and not talking to her. He was angry with her for something she hadn't done and she was also angry for the fact that he didn't trust her. Did he really think she would have an affair with the person who hurt her the most? She was in time to hear the pastor quote Isaiah 2:22 in which God cautioned his people not to put their trust in mere human beings since they are as frail as the breath. What good are they? Did he just do that, Beth thought as she huffed at his audacity. Since he was chairing the service, he was seated at the front, yet when the pastor came to that part, Rob had stared at her as if the minister was talking about her. She chuckled at how petty he could be and continued to listen to the minister as he wrapped up his preaching. A few hymns were sung after wards before they dismissed. This would be their last day of the conference and she already dreaded the journey ahead with Rob who was turning out to be surly like long dead Lisa. "Beth," Rob called as she walked out of the building. She turned only to see her view blocked by her mother's best friend Courtney. "Beth dear." She greeted as she hugged and kissed her. Beth noticed Rob moving away with Pastor Wilson and wondered what they would be talking about.

Rob was wondering the same as Pastor Wilson led him to his office. He settled down on the chair and waited. They had shared a few pleasantries before since the man was well known by his father.

"What is this am hearing about you leaving the ministry?" He asked as he leaned back on the chair. He was shocked when he heard the news as he thought Rob was far better off than his good for nothing son who was now tarnishing his name. Rob cleared his throat before finally stating, "I felt I was being a hypocrite, that's why. Throughout I had been preaching to people about forgiving those who wronged them and yet when I discovered my late wife infidelity, I failed to do that. " Pastor Wilson sighed, "That's why we are called earthen vessels after all. The story isn't about us at the end of the day, but about God the Father, our creator, His Son and the Holy Spirit gifted unto us. God knows how fragile we are and that is the beauty of it all. Him working in us as we boldly go to Him with all our weaknesses and He fashions us into something beautiful by his Holy Spirit. What happened to you doesn't make you into a hypocrite. The fact that you are aware that you failed to forgive, makes you trust more in God's forgiveness for you which will empower you to forgive. Now you can empathize with those who face the challenge and show them that they need forgiveness that comes from God to be able to forgive their neighbor." Rob nodded as the old preacher said the few words. How many times had he told others to not focus on themselves but on the grace of God. Yet he had been preoccupied with focusing on himself and the injustice that Lisa had done. He smiled as he thought on how God in his mercy had revealed that part in time and he was learning to live with the knowledge that even though a human being might betray him, God never changed his position and still loved him. Pastor Wilson chuckled before continuing, "The reason why I called you is because of Elizabeth. Heard she is now your wife?" Rob nodded wondering what the old man wanted to say.

"She is a good girl. I was disappointed the day I found out about what the board of women did to her pertaining to her relationship with Jeffrey. By the time I heard the new they had already left. No one was aware of my son's behaviour until a few girls brave enough started to talk." He heaved a weary sigh and Rob could see that the man was rather conflicted and saddened as he talked. "It is commendable that you married her, despite her history. She has always been nothing but exemplary in her conduct. I know my son seeing the wrong path his taking, might want to make trouble for both of you in future, so I made him do something for me as an ultimatum." He stood up and moved to the file cabinet where he took out a folder and settled down again before handing it to Rob. Robin opened the folder and read out the document in it. His eyes widened as he read on. Pastor Wilson had made his son give up any rights or claims he might have over Beth's son. "I know this might seem extreme. Jeffrey admitted that he had toyed with the young lady but I will not let him take the opportunity to destroy the good thing she has now. He denied her initially hence he doesn't in anyway deserve to be called a father, whether now on in future." Rob was out of words as the preacher spoke. He had caught a few whispers here and there about Jeffrey with women and how they were out for blood as more came forward. Was it possible that Beth had innocently answered the door and Jeff budged into the room? He thought on how relieved she had seemed when he got in. As he stared at the Pastor who seemed saddened by the whole matter; he realized how wrong he had been. Beth wasn't Lisa after all. He stood up and shook the man's hand, grateful for what he had done for them. Ryan was his son and forever will be as he knew only him as his father. "Greet your parents for me. We might not get to meet after the evening service. So have a safe journey." He smiled as Rob nodded and walked out of the office.

"BETH" ROB CALLED AS he got into their hotel room. He chuckled when he noticed her sleeping on the bed. She must have dozed off; he thought as he moved towards her and saw the bible and notepad with a pen on her side. He read what she had written, some few affirmation verses on who she was in Christ. He removed the things on the bed and put them aside on the headboard before lying next to her and watching her sleep. She was beautiful. He lovingly brushed off the hair that had fallen over her face as she slowly opened her eyes. "Sorry, didn't mean to wake you up"

She smiled, "Its ok." Beth stared back at her husband who only had love shining for her in his eyes. She chuckled as she wondered on what they had been fighting about in the first place. Rob cleared his throat before reaching out on the headboard. "I had a chat with Pastor Wilson, more like he talked and I listened." She giggled when she heard that, since Pastor Wilson had always been talkative. "Here." He handed her the folder with the document. Beth opened it and he could see her eyes widening up as she read it, the same way he had reacted. "Hey." He whispered as he pulled her into a hug, already seeing the tears fall down her face. He lightly brushed them away with the thumb before stating, "He said, Jeffrey admitted that he had toyed with you, but wouldn't allow him to make trouble for you, that's why he made him sign this." Beth dragged out a long heavy sigh finally feeling the heavy load lift from her shoulders. The fact that Jeffrey had admitted that she wasn't obsessed with him as he had claimed before. "Hey," he tilted her head by the chin, "Thought you would be celebrating that he admitted you are not what he had tried to portray you as, a loose woman." She swatted his arm and giggled. "How did you know that," she was stunned by how he seemed to read what she was thinking so easily. "One of those occupational hazard," he grinned. "At times innocent girls get toyed with and wonder why boys act the way they do after they give in. they place the blame on themselves. Am I loose, did I give in easily; is that the reason why he left me?" She hugged him, relishing his warmth. "You are a good man, Rob." She whispered as he tilted her head back again and lovingly kissed her. "And you are a good woman, Elizabeth Parker. One who deserves all the happiness in the world," he replied and continued to kiss her to her hearts content.

Chapter 12

BETH WALKED HOME FEELING excited and exhausted at the same time. The event was a month away now, very close and the children had to be properly prepared. She loved being a Sunday school teacher cum music teacher. Especially when the children's sweet voices blended together as they sung out the Christmas carols, it always managed to make her day. The costumes were already fixed for the Christmas play, and she couldn't wait to see their delighted tiny faces as they tried them on the next day. She decided to pass by her in-laws place and take her two children before she could go home. The nanny had been feeling poorly and she hoped she would get well soon. She opened the door and came into the living room. Her mother in law who was usually to be found sipping tea on the recliner wasn't there. Where was the maid, she wondered as she moved to the corridor. Maybe she would be in the guest bedroom with the children. Ryan could sit and was rather troublesome since he had a tendency of throwing himself on the bed. Hence they never made him sit on the floor; unless some cushions and blankets were placed on it, in case he decided to do his small falling episode and hit his head on floor. Moving along the corridor she could hear voices coming from the study as she slightly opened the door and was shocked to see a gathering oblivious to her.

"Is this true Rob," Tina muttered as she looked with pleading eyes on her son to deny the matter. Charles was scowling at the corner not caring on the theatrics of the woman. "I found out the day we buried her. It is true" he whispered and placed his head in his hands. He looked weary, tired of even fighting. "It can't be, no I will not accept this" she shouted as Charles growled. "Whether you like it or not Mrs. Parker, that is my child and I am here to take her."

"Tensions appear to be high," Nancy nervously said, "I think the child is better off with me while you sort out your differences, I wouldn't want my daughter's memory to be dragged in the mud" Charles was more than relieved, as long as Penny was out of Rob's house he would be at peace. "It's for the best" he growled as Mrs. Richards said to Tina, "Give me the child." A sob was heard from the door as everyone turned to find Beth standing right inside the library. She stared at all of them, shock still evident in her face before she turned and walked away.

"Beth," Tina called, following behind. She hadn't expected her to show up early and witness the drama playing out. "Beth dear." Beth ignored her mother in law as she walked out of the house. How could they do this to her and poor Penny? Tina managed to hold her hand before she could open the door to her house. "Beth, there is nothing we can do." She scowled at her mother in law and spat out, "You gave away my daughter without even talking to me and you say they is nothing you can do about it." She yanked the door open and got into her house. She needed to do something, she thought as she moved to her bedroom. "Beth, we want to avoid scandal as we possibly can. You will have Penny with you in no time, when things have been sorted out."

"Wow, mother in law, you are surely the woman of the year. When you gave Penny to me you said I was now her mother, but now you make decisions behind my back. Did you think about how I would feel about this, did you think about how Penny will feel. None of you did. All you thought about was how to avoid a scandal. You didn't even call me to give me a chance to have a say on my daughter. Today you have proven that I mean nothing to you."

"Beth you can't mean that" Tina softly chided as she stared at her daughter in-laws hurt face. ""Yes I mean it. If you will excuse me. I would like to pack up now." Tina shrugged her shoulders in defeat, having followed Beth to her room. She didn't know how she could comfort the distressed mother. She sighed and decided to walk away. Pack up, did Beth mean she was leaving Rob. She was just in time to see Rob get into the house with Ryan. "Rob, Beth is angry and she might leave, stop her" she muttered as she got her other grandchild and he rushed to his wife. "Beth" he called. Her clothes were now scattered over the bed not yet packed as she wept and walked around the wardrobe to get a suitcase. He pulled her into his arms, comforting her. "How could you do this to me" she wailed louder. "You accepted Ryan as yours and would fight tooth and nail for him, how can you not do the same for Penny. She is our daughter Rob."

"It's a bit complicated," he whispered to which she pulled out of his embrace. "You might not like to be Penny's dad but I am her mother" she pointed at him as she stamped her feet at the same time. "Couldn't you think of that at least and fought back. Complicated my foot." she went towards her bed and shoved her clothes into the suitcase. Rob grabbed her hands before she could pack any further, "Beth you can't leave me, please don't do this." She finally stared at him and could see he was hurting also. She wearily sighed before slumping on the bed. She still loved the man but right now she didn't like him at all since he had failed to fight for them. "I am moving to the guest room. Bring my son there or you also intend to give him away freely like you did his sister."

Rob was relieved at hearing her say she wasn't leaving. She walked out of the room still angry but the thought that she would not leave produced a slight smile on his sad countenance.

BETH DID NOT COME OUT of her room and played around with Ryan. She was angry at the decision that the adults had taken not even thinking about her feelings. The woman who had created this whole confusion wasn't alive for her to rant on. After feeding Ryan, she decided to get up and go and prepare supper. She peeked through their bedroom and Rob wasn't in it. As she walked to the kitchen, she wondered where he had gone to. She knew she had been unfair in being angry with him at the same time she was right. He was just taking an unconcerned stand when it came to Penny. As if he didn't care what happened to her. She sniffed the air of the kitchen and caught a whiff of aroma before opening the warmer. A closed plate was in there with a message of top. *Sorry love for everything. I love you and my children very much. I know you might be angry now, but I promise to get our daughter. I will be back. Love you always.* It read. She brushed off the tears from her eyes and settled down on the kitchen chair. She removed the lid. He had prepared French toast, roasted beef and some greens on the side. Always a better cook than her, she thought as she slowly ate her supper.

ROB GOT INTO THE PRIVATE lounge of the bar with a few misgivings. He had made a promise to himself and his wife that he would not come back to the bar and drown himself in a bottle. He felt that he was not being truthful even though this was for another cause and he wouldn't be drinking at all. This had to be done and he knew he would only get to see Rob there. He removed his hat and nodded to the bartender who indicated where Charles sat already full in his cups. He moved towards him and watched his best friend raise his head and glower at him.

"What brings you here Pastor Rob" he slurred, angrily standing up so he could leave. "Don't" Rob stayed him with his hand. "I just need us to talk. Please."

Charles finally settled down and listened. "Why are you doing this"? Rob asked. "Penny is my daughter, that's why" he snorted and gulped the scotch in his glass. He motioned the bartender to pour more. "How do you know she is yours, it's not like Lisa was honest with any of us." Charles scowled at that and growled, "Lisa was a good woman. I loved her but you and her mother didn't want us to be together."

"I didn't know and you never said a word about it," Rob grumbled, "I would have left her if only you had told me."

"Like you left Beth," Charles scowled as they both knew that is not what happened. "With Beth it's different and you know it."

"How is that any different? Hmmm." He loathed having this conversation and stood up. "Please" Rob pleaded with his eyes. He wanted to revenge to the man who took away his happiness at the same time seeing him saddened in that manner took away his bravado and only left him feeling empty. "Beth didn't love you. That's why it's different" Rob finally said. "I admit I suspected that Lisa might have loved someone else other than me, but I thought it was just my mind playing tricks on me, especially when she agreed to get married to me. Both of you never said anything, and to think Charles you were my friend. Now you come and take away Penny from the home she knows, why now."

Charles slouched his shoulders in defeat before replying "Misery wants a friend. I was a coward and I failed to stand by her when she needed me the most. Her mother warned me off. Do you know what it feels like to be always on the outside looking in? I distanced myself from my family but still I never could be good enough." He motioned the bartender to pour in more of the scotch. Rob shook his head before helping his friend to stand. "Let me take you home," he stated before he held him so he couldn't topple down and they left for the parking lot.

Chapter 13

A KNOCK WAS HEARD AS Beth groggily opened her eyes. She reached out to the other side of the bed and remembered she had vacated her bedroom. She got up from the bed wondering who could be visiting in the middle of the night. She wore a robe over her nighty before she went to answer the door. Where was Robin since the bed was still made up and he was not yet back. She reached the door and shouted, "Who is it?"

"It's Mr. Richards dear." What could Lisa's father be looking for at this hour? Thinking of Penny she quickly opened the door and let him in. "How can I be of help."

The old man coughed and cleared his throat before saying, "Penny needs you. She has been crying and we are all failing to quiet her down. She hasn't drunk any milk and..." She didn't let him finish as she told him she was coming back. She packed up a few things before she got Ryan and swiftly moved to where the old man still stood. "I am set, let's go." He helped her with the baby seat as they left for his house. Her heart broke as she could hear Penny crying weakly and the grandmother trying to shush her when they got into the house. "Give her to me," she advised.

Nancy seemed reluctant until her husband nudged her and she gave Beth the baby.

They indicated a room for her, where Ryan was now lying on the bed and she settled on the edge of it. "I am here now my princess," she whispered. "Mommy will take care of you." Penny looked pale as she placed her little mouth on her nipple. She wasn't suckling but instead continued with her soft whimpers. Since she had once done that before, Beth stood up and put her on the shoulders, moving around the room. She finally settled down again and this time squirted the milk on her mouth. It trickled to her tiny mouth and finally her mouth opened. There was no need for her to cox her to suckle as she lustily pulled her breast and drank her fill. Beth chuckled at that. "Naughty girl throwing your tantrum again," she whispered as she continued feeding her and lay on the bed next to Ryan who was soundly asleep unaware of the events taking place around him. Finally Penny fell asleep. She tucked both babies and left the room. She was shocked to find Mrs. Richards still awake. "Thought you had already gone to bed" she whispered. "I didn't." They was a slight pause before Beth said, "I will pump some more breast milk for Penny, just squirt it over her mouth if she refuses the bottle. That taste of the first drop will make her drink."

"Always temperamental like the mother," Nancy huffed as Beth chuckled. "Thank you again for doing this" she softly spoke. Beth nodded. "It's no bother, I am her mother after all and mothers know what's best for their daughters."

Nancy clutched at her throat as if she had seen a ghost as Beth's eyes widened and she swiftly moved to the woman who looked like she was about to faint. "Are you ok, Mrs. Richards?" she asked as she helped her sit back on the couch. "I am fine," she whispered as she thought on what Beth had said. Seeing her concerned expression she realized that Beth didn't know anything about her relation to Lisa. It was after she managed to slow down her pounding heart, she instructed Beth where she could find everything she needed before she left for bed. Beth went to the kitchen, prepared a cup of tea before she took the empty milk bottles and moved to the room. She hadn't looked at the room properly before but as she surveyed it; she noticed some Pics of Lisa and moved towards the closet. As she had guessed, this had been Lisa's room. Everything appeared to be the same way it might have been the times Lisa visited. She opened the chest of drawers and they still held her clothes. Neatly folded as if waiting for their owner to wear them. "What a mess Lisa, can't you give me a clue to who you truly were? She thought aloud as she lay back on the bed and immediately fell asleep.

"HONEY WHERE HAVE YOU been?" Rick asked concern evident in his voice as he moved from the couch, having heard the sound of the door. Ever since he arrived back home around 3am after having listened to Charles sad love story, only to find his wife gone, he had been worried sick. He couldn't get hold of her over the phone and he had nearly knocked off his parent's door in a panic. His mother advised he wait for her, as he had been about to drive over to her mother's place. "I was out taking care of my daughter, or you don't want me to do that also," she angrily said and sauntered towards the guest room where she laid Ryan on the bed. He thought the note he left might have pacified her, apparently not. "You should have left a note, was worried sick" Rob lounged over the door fearing to get in as she looked mighty pissed. Beth was feeling grumpy after having left her daughter. It was tearing her apart the fact that, Penny might never have a normal family after all this. She didn't mean to lash out at Rob but she just wanted to scream and hail her anger at someone. She found nothing to help her or a clue that Lisa might have left. Only a normal bedroom for a lady with no secrets hidden under the bed or boxes. "Like you were too worried for me and took the time to tell me that you were giving away my daughter." She moved towards the door still spiting fire and shut it in his face. He sighed and walked away, failing to find a way on how he could reach her. He needed his Beth back.

BETH BREAST FED RYAN and placed him on the bed with a few pillows to lean on, though he could sit on his own. She placed a few toys for him to play with before moving to the wardrobe. Rob had kept some of the things that belonged to Lisa in the guest room for Penny when she was all grown up. She took the box, moved towards the bed and settled down. 'You were such a cruel woman to have done this,' she muttered under her breath as she went through the things. A few trophies, her year book, some framed photos, all impersonal and none actually showing the kind of woman she had been. She sighed out loud and moved towards the wardrobe again. She would need an extra blanket since Ryan will be sleeping in her room. The nursery was far away as it adjoined the bedroom she had vacated. She pulled off the cover from the top shelf and two diaries fell along with it. Staring at them disbelief in her eyes, she thought on how this was the answer to her problems. She had a few misgivings over reading through a dead woman's deepest secrets. *Get a grip of yourself Bethy, this is for Penny.* She stared at the other pink diary, the bigger one of the two and placed it back on the shelf. It's not like Lisa would have written any deep secrets there, since it didn't have a lock. Taking the smaller one, she moved to the edge of the bed and settled down. She needed the key. She ruffled through the chest of drawers and remembered that Rob had handed her a set of keys when they started staying together. She went to her room, collected them and right along with the house keys, was a smaller key that would fit on the diary. She nearly squealed in delight when it easily slid in the lock and opened. She was doing all this for her daughter; she justified in her mind as she opened the book and started reading. Since it didn't have any dates marking it, she riffled through some entries looking for something that would stand out. She came to one and paused on it. It read, *Dear diary*

There is a new girl in town that everyone keeps on talking about, Elizabeth Martins. Her heart skipped a beat at the fact that Lisa wrote about her and almost shut the diary again. She curbed the impulse and read on, *she is pretty but not that pretty yet everyone seems to be crazy about her including my husband. He dots over her as if she is the only woman to be having a child out of wedlock. I find myself becoming jealous over his attention towards her that I don't know what to do. Should I tell him to stay away from her, or I will push him further into her arms.*

She shut the diary shocked. That was silly, how could Lisa have thought Rob would leave her for the new girl in town. Her reasoning wasn't making any sense. She flipped other pages and came to the part where one had been torn off. She guessed it might be the one that Rob read, and read the next entry. *Dear Diary.*

I find myself missing C more and more. Was it right for me to have listened to my mother and left him because he didn't have the loving family that R has. Today is my wedding day and I don't know if I should choose love for my baby or the man I love. If only C had been clear of his intentions, then I wouldn't be struggling like this to decide. He isn't willing to fight for us and tell R that we are in love. Conflicted.

Seriously, couldn't you just have numbered the pages, Beth rolled her eyes. And what was up with the colors of the pages, some were of white paper, sky blue, and pink. She put the diary aside not wanting to read further about Lisa's love story and on how she so much missed C. As it now turned out she knew who C was since he had taken Penny away from them. She wouldn't have thought that of him. Charles had seemed to her like a take charge kind of person and not at all how Lisa described him as undecided. He had been willing to marry her after all with her son. Duty still called and they were still preparing for the Christmas festival. She got up and decided to get ready before she left for church. She hoped she would see Penny also at night, since she feared Charles might not take too kindly to hearing the news that she still stuck around the child.

Chapter 14

HER DAY WITH THE KIDS managed to take away the woes she had of her family life not being complete. Her mother and aunt also visited her while she was still at church and had a chat with her. She felt refreshed as she walked back home while pushing Ryan in the stroller. She believed things would work out well at the end. Her mother in law had been at the church also having a meeting with the married women. She had popped into the hall where the children were singing, looking contrite over not considering her feelings. She chuckled when she thought about it as the woman had settled down with her and told her how much she loved her as her own daughter and had thought it best to keep things under wraps as they possibly could. Beth realized that she was being genuine and the fact that if rumors began to circulate, they will be back to square one, with Rob maybe resorting to drinking, while she moaned over what could have been. Leave it to the old woman to paint out the worst case scenario.

"Hey honey," Rob greeted as he came out of the house and took Ryan into his arms. She folded the baby stroller and followed him. "I was thinking, that we go together to see Penny."

"You really would do that," she asked, shocked as he chuckled. "She is my daughter after all. I spoke with Nancy. So will be having dinner at their place." She gushed at that. Meaning she would stay longer with Penny. "Go and freshen up, I will take care of Ryan" he advised as she lunged towards him almost toppling him over with his son. "Thank you" she whispered before pasting a kiss on his mouth and moving away. If only he had known that would take away her anger, he would have done that earlier, he thought, shaking his head and moving to children's nursery.

LAUGHTER COULD BE HEARD in the Richards home as the people who sat over dinner joked and retold stories. The children were in the living room, also having a conversation of their own, or Ryan did most of the unintelligibly talk while Penny played with her toys, lying on the piled up blanket on the carpeted floor. Beth had cushioned it for the kids incase Ryan decided to do his falling fit on the ground hence he could land on something soft. "This has been rather nice, thank you for this" Nancy whispered as she wiped off the tears at the corner of her eye. Having Rob around reminded her of Lisa and how so good together they had been. She didn't regret forcing her daughter to get married to him. That good for nothing Charles would have ruined her life like what he was doing now, ruining Penny's life. She would have to come clean and tell them everything, but right now she was content with having their company. She knew that she alone would clear the confusion, but she wasn't willing to part with everything she worked for if the truth came out. Beth appeared not to be aware also on her relation with Penny. How did things get this far? She wondered as she took a sip on her water. "Nance," her husband stared at her concerned as her expression had seemed vacant for a while. She hadn't noticed that Beth had cleared the plates already and Rob was now with the children. He moved towards her and asked, "Are you going to tell them the truth. Don't you think this fuss has gone on long enough." She scowled at him before standing up.

"Rob you can take Penny home for today," she advised him and watched his face widen with a smile. Beth came back from the kitchen and hugged her. "Thank you so much Mrs. Richards, she remarked elated at the prospect of having Penny under her roof. "Nancy is fine" she stated addressing the young woman before moving towards the couch. Her husband was still looking at her disapprovingly. Beth went back to finish off the dishes before they could leave with her two children for home.

CHARLES CURSED UNDER his breath as he saw Rob's car parked outside the Richards home. He drove past it and parked his across the road where he could view what was happening. From where he was, he saw four adults come out of the house, happy as their voices drifted to him. Rob was carrying Ryan while Beth carried Penny. Thinking she would hand over the child back to the grandmother as they chatted on the patio, he was shocked when he saw her take Penny to the car. No this can't be happening, he thought. He had been ready to give up on the whole idea of making Rob suffer yet seeing Nancy had gone behind his back, infuriated him further. Its time he took away his daughter for good from Rob as well as the grandmother. He watched them drive off and the old couple got into the house before sliding off from his car and moving towards the house. He used to meet Lisa in their library since the window could be pried open easily. The street was quiet with no other people moving around; hence he moved to the back of the house, opened the window and got in. He settled on one of the chairs and waited.

"I CAN'T BELIEVE MY princess is home where she is meant to be," Beth sniffled as she tucked Penny in and placed a kiss on her forehead. Rob was done with Ryan. He looked up to find Beth brushing off the tears as if they were a menace. He moved towards and hugged her as she drew closer and wept. "Hush now love," he whispered. "Penny is home. Hopefully tomorrow's news would be favorable."

She stared at him enquiringly as he chuckled, "I took Penny's brush for strands of hair and made a few calls so I could get the DNA results. I can't take the uncertainty of it all" he admitted as she returned to hugging him. "I am sure, Penny is yours. She doesn't look at all like Charles."

"Looks can be deceiving" he muttered under his breath. "Don't be negative Pastor Robin." She stated with conviction as she looked up to him again. She could see the hurt in his eyes and wished she had been understanding over his plight and not lashing out at him in the first place. He leaned over for a kiss and after they had drawn apart said, "You don't know how I have missed you pumpy. These two days have been torture."

"Sorry for being so harsh with you." He shrugged his shoulders and said with a laugh, "I am rather used to you baring your fangs all the time at least I get to have the best make up sex afterwards." Beth huffed and pinched him for saying that. He picked her up and slowly kissed her before moving towards their room. "You see what I meant. Putty in my hands," he chuckled as she softly glowered at him and wrapped her arms tightly around him before playfully biting him on the neck.

Chapter 15

NEIL RICHARDS WAS FEELING restless as his wife slept soundly next to him. For how long would Nancy continue hiding the truth? So what if she lost everything, they still had each other. Who knows, maybe by speaking the truth she might gain a family at the end. He breathed a heavy weary sigh before getting up from bed. What he needed was a drink and a good book to take off his mind from thinking about the problems at hand. He walked towards the library and flipped the switch on the wall. Funny, he thought he had left the decanter half full when he went to bed. He shrugged off his shoulders dismissively and reached out to the small cabinet where he stored the rest of it. As he stood up straight and looked at the mirror, he was met by blood shot eyes angrily glaring at him before everything went dark.

Nancy rolled over the bed and reached out to the other side. Where had Neil gone to and at such a late hour, she wondered as she got up from bed and slowly walked towards the library. She hoped he wasn't drinking himself to sleep as she could see the light filtering through the corridor. She opened the door and was met by a smirking young man who greeted, "welcome Nancy, time you joined the party." She froze as Charles shifted and she saw her husband on the chair, lying limply and a trickle of blood oozed from his forehead. "What have you done," she screamed, rushing to her husband and shaking him. "He is not dead," he muttered before barking "sit down." Nancy hadn't noticed that Charles was holding anything until she angrily looked up to retort and found herself looking at the end of the barrel of a gun.

She nervously settled down and looked into his blood shot eyes. "What do you want?" He sneered, "My daughter of course. Where is she?" The old woman glared at him before speaking in a soothing manner a contrast to the glare. "It is late and she is resting. Why don't you come and see her in the afternoon?"

"Nancy, bring my daughter here so I can see her." He was now settled opposite them and he shifted the barrel and aimed at her husband. "She is at Rob's house," she faintly stated as Charles used his other hand to scratch his ear. "Hmmm." He hummed and scratched on his ear as if removing dust so to hear clearly. "She is at Rob's house." She spoke louder and watched him sneer. "And why would you do a dastard thing like that." Nancy was already regretting not having told the truth as she realized that Charles was out for blood. He couldn't be reasoned with. He seemed drunk and angry, a combination that spelt out trouble. "Rob is her father." Charles stared at her not believing a word. He laughed and stared into her eyes. "You know that is a lie. Penny is my child. Lisa told me when she fell pregnant." Nancy was trembling as Charles cocked the gun still pointing at her husband. "Lisa lost the child the day after the wedding." Charles abruptly stood up and menacingly moved toward the woman who flinched as he approached. He leaned over and she could smell the fumes of alcohol emanating from his whole being. "Why are you lying?"

She could feel a trickle of sweat on her forehead and neck. Her husband was breathing steady on her side but not yet conscious. "I am telling the truth. Penny is Rob's daughter.

Charles moved back, cradling his head and circling his forehead with the gun, "You are lying, are you willing to bank your husband's life on such a lie," he harshly stated before moving to the old man and grabbing him from the chair. He shook him up as he was limp in his arms before placing the gun on his forehead.

"Charles, please," Nancy screamed terrified. He shoved the old man back to the seat, before glaring with hatred on the woman who had taken his Lisa away from him. "Why didn't you mention that to Rob before?" Nancy clamped her mouth shut as he moved towards her and pointed the gun in her face. "Why dear Nancy?" The woman though scared seemed to be resolved to her fate as if not concerned if she died. He went back to her husband and noticed how terrified she was. So she would die with the secret if the threat was on her life but if her husband was in harm's way she would try to protect him. He chuckled. "Beth,"

"Go on"

"Beth is Lisa's young sister," she finally blurted out. He looked at her confused. "What does Beth have to do with any of this?"

"My husband left half of the ranch to her. Lisa's half will belong to Penny when she comes of age." He finally understood and roared with laughter. Neil stirred and he slowly opened his eyes to be met by those of his terrified wife. "Ooh I see. So you don't want Beth to know that she is Lisa's sister. She will get the remaining half and they own everything while you have nothing."

He paced around the library as he contemplated his next move. "How long were you going to keep up this ruse?" Neil shook his head as he didn't want Nancy to answer that. He winced as Charles turned to face him "welcome back to the land of the living. You are just in time to hear about your wife's mechanizing."

"I would have gone with the truth to my grave."

"You still can," he chuckled as he handed her the phone. "Just call Rob and tell him I want my daughter."

"But she is not," she protested as Charles roared with laughter again. "Rob doesn't know that. I get the daughter and the proceeds for half the ranch, you keep the other half," he sneered.

"Don't," Neil weakly advised as he stared at his wife. "Can we call later on; they will be suspicious if I was to call now." She looked at the clock on the wall, it was now 4am. Charles sighed; he didn't want the man also passing out any moment since he appeared to be important to Nancy. "Take the first aid kit and take care of that gush on the forehead" he advised before settling down on the seat opposite them. "No funny business or he is dead."

Chapter 16

BETH CAME OUT OF THE bath giggling after taking a bath with her randy husband. She dried her hair with a towel as she walked to the dresser and settled on the chair. The kids will still be sleeping, so she had time to be presentable that is if Rob didn't start another love session. He walked into the room with a white towel tied around his waist and winked. "What's up for the day," he asked as he walked towards the wardrobe where he got the jeans and t-shirt out of the closet and placed them on the bed before walking towards her and hugging her from her back. She could see the desire in his eyes as he stared at her in the mirror. "Thought you were going to work Mr. you might have left the ministry but we still need money for things around the house." She grinned as he turned her over on her seat and noisily kissed her. "I still have to pick the package in an hours time." The answer to all their questions that would clear the confusion once and for all. She looked at the alarm clock on the dresser before stating. "One hour," he winked "One hour" before swiftly picking her from the chair and moving towards the bed. She grumbled as he shoved aside the clothes thinking she would have to iron them again after being creased, while he shrugged his shoulders and continued to kiss her senselessly. They were both breathless when they came up as she shut his mouth with her hand. They heard the sound again. The kids were up. Sighing loudly they got off the bed. Apparently they weren't going to have their one hour after all. She rushed to their cots, where she found both competing over who cried the loudest. "Ryan you naughty boy," she remarked as he had the audacity to gurgle at being caught on a lie since no tears were rolling down his tiny cheeks. She plucked out Penny from her cradle and swiftly changed her wet nappy, before attending to Ryan. Rob came into the nursery dressed in the black t-shirt and jeans, at least they hadn't creased up having been thrown carelessly onto the carpeted floor, she thought as he got Ryan from her and they moved towards the kitchen. Both the children had high backed chairs; hence Ryan was placed in one of the chairs since he could now sit while Penny remained in her father's lap. Beth got busy preparing breakfast as she chatted with her husband. After they were done, he asked worriedly looking at her, "Will you be fine."

"Don't be silly. I will be. Just go and take the results. I am sure Nancy will take Penny later on during the day." He stared at the wrist watch, it was now 7 am and the lab would be open at 7:30, he really needed to know. He got up from the chair with Penny in his arms. Kissed her before giving her to the mother, kissed the mother and Ryan. "Later love" he said before leaving for the lab in town. He was just in time to find Mr. Wilkinson getting boxes from his truck and getting into his shop. The town was not yet in full swing as people started coming in after 8.00am. He greeted the deli owner before helping him with the boxes. He tended to prepare some of the burgers at his home; hence Rob chuckled when he received a paperback full of the beef burger and chicken pies. "For Beth, I know she loves them," the old man winked before getting behind the counter. Rob grinned and waved to the old man. He left the deli and walked to the lab that was at the corner of the street. "Rob," Joey greeted as he came in. "Fresh from the market," he continued with a laugh. "I knew you wouldn't stay away for long."

"Thanks a lot Joey, you don't know how much this means to me," he looked at him appreciatively as Joey had gone beyond in order for him to have the results. Their small town got things from the major towns a week later. Three days had seemed impossible yet it was done. "No problem Pastor, anything for you." Joey nodded his head. Rob came out of the lab and got into his pick up truck before nervously opening the envelope after placing the paperback on the other seat. For a while he was in a daze, after reading the results. Penny was his daughter, Penny was his daughter. The phone chimed and he looked at the message. One word from Nancy, help.

IT WAS FIVE MINUTES after Rob had left that Beth heard the phone ringing and picked it up. Nancy sounded strained out of sorts as she told Beth to bring Penny over. "Rob has left for a while. Will bring her over when he is back." She advised as Nancy sighed. They was a long pause as if she had hung up yet Beth could hear her breathing. "Ok, see you when Rob is back." Nancy finally stated and hung up. Beth wondered what the woman was up to. Since Penny had fallen asleep after breakfast while Ryan was attempting to move with his butt while seated on a blanket, she decided to take the Pink diary and read it instead. The color coded one just wasn't working for her, as she had read about Lisa's love for Charles and almost wept for poor Rob. She hoped it didn't have the drivel the first one had. She opened and sniffed the lavender scent that Lisa used to wear. *Dear angel. It's been a month since you left and I sorely miss you. I am sorry for not being the best mom I could be and protecting you. You were my world and I feel devoid, lost without you.* Beth read out the words confused and wondering if she had missed something.

At times I am angered at the fact that I lost you immediately after my first night. He took you away from me. Dear old Nancy insisted on performing my marital duties on my first night so it wouldn't be suspicious when you came along. I was forced and the next day I lost you. Beth could see the pen imprint as at this time Lisa might have been pressing hard on the book as she wrote. *I had to lie to him and inform him I was in my menses when I lost you and unknown to him I was grieving. To my mother, husband you were just a clot of blood that caused me to be irritable. Yet to me you had been everything. I forsook the man I loved so you could have a better future. The concerned husband that my mother sort wasn't concerned at all when he suggested I resume my marital duties a week after you were gone.*

Couldn't he see that I grieved, I hurt and as usual dear old Nancy covered the issue by stating that it was just hormones? Bah. The nerve of the woman. Poor Rob, she thought. Lisa lost the child that's what kept on ringing in Beth's ears as she flipped through the other pages. She needed her word to show that Penny was Rob's daughter.

Today I visited the doctor and as suspected I am pregnant again. Everyone is elated except I feel dead on the inside. I don't want to live but I am too scared to die. Rob is over the moon and dear old Nancy is already contemplating on the things that you need. Dear Nancy who stated that I could replace a child with another as if I was getting a new set of shoes, dear Nancy who acts like a caring mother but all she thinks about is her reputation. The woman doesn't care for me neither did she care for my unborn child. Will she care for this new one then, ironic indeed?

Beth had abruptly stood up from the couch as realization dawned. Why didn't people see that before, Penny was conceived three months after Rob and Lisa had been married?

Nancy knew that, why didn't she mention it before? She heard the sound of the door closing and hurriedly rushed to the kitchen as her husband got in with a smile on his face. "Penny is yours, mine" they each said in unison as they stared at each other in disbelief. She rushed into his arms and he held her tightly and settled with her on the couch. "How did you know? He asked as she giggled and at the same time tears streamed down her face. Only she could pull such a fit. "Lisa wrote everything down in her diary; Rob pulled out the results and handed them to Beth who read them aloud. "we have to go," he seemed worried and she wondered why. "Nancy sent a cryptic message, just one word, help." I managed to inform the police before I left town, they should be by their house by now. Beth clutched at her throat, long forgotten the good news as now her question to why her voice sounded strained was answered. "Do you think Charles is over there." Rob nodded before picking up Ryan from his blanket. "I will be waiting in the car.' He had driven like a maniac after the message, worried he might find trouble in his home. He was relieved to find Beth ok, all he had to do was leave her and the kids at his parents place, he just couldn't place them in any kind of danger. Beth came outside and closed the door. She was shocked when Rob drove the car to his parents place. "No I am not letting you go alone," she advised. "When Nancy called she wanted Penny."

"Hey love," he cradled her face in his hands, "I need you and the children to be safe. Maybe it's nothing but an old senile woman just playing games."

"You know it's not. We can leave the children with your parents and we go together." Rob sighed and nodded his head. His mother was already walking towards the car, worry evident on her face. "What's going on," Tina asked as Rob answered, "will answer all your questions when we get back. He came out of the car and carried Ryan while his mother carried Penny. "Take care of yourself and Beth, please" she whispered and hugged him after he had made sure the children were well settled. He nodded before leaving the house. By the time they got to the house it seemed a lot of activity was already going on. An ambulance was already on standby while Charles was being shoved out of the house handcuffed. "What happened," Rob asked one of his friends Henry whom he had spoken to at the police station. Henry explained what had transpired before chuckling, "Nancy did it all, she stalled for time till Charles curbed in to exhaustion. Mr. Richards is hurt though." As he spoke they watched him being wheeled to the ambulance. Beth was already at Nancy side, helping her walk to the ambulance where she got in after her husband. "Thank you so much," Rob stated as he shook Henry's hand and left for his car, knowing Beth would come there so they followed the couple to the hospital.

"This could have ended badly if Charles had been a criminal," Rob spoke on a sober note when Beth got into the car and they trailed behind the ambulance. "What do you think is going to happen to him." he shrugged his shoulders, "he held them at gun point and also assaulted Mr. Richards, the judgment might go both ways."

"It's a pity" she quietly remarked and looked out of the window as the car moved along. One thing still niggled at her, why Nancy never cleared the whole matter the first time Charles demanded to take Penny from Rob.

Chapter 17

ROSE AND ELLEN BURST into the waiting room and hugged Beth and Rob. Tina had called them and updated them on what had happened. The nurse motioned for them to get into the ward as Rob pulled Beth and let the adults get in first. She looked enquiringly at him as he shook his head. He wanted an explanation; hence that's why he had stopped Beth from getting in first. Nancy had known but still failed to clear her daughter's name. Ellen and Rose came out of the ward and hugged them before they left for home. They got into the ward and Beth moved to Mr. Richards side who grasped her hand. "How are you feeling?" Beth asked concerned. The gash had been stitched and bandaged. "Fine dear." He smiled. Rob looked at Nancy settled on the chair beside her husband's bed as she failed to meet his eyes. Her husband nudged her with his elbow before she coughed clearing her throat. "Rob, Beth, I am sorry for what you had to go through because of my selfishness" she muttered. "It is well Nancy," Beth cut in soothingly as her husband stared disapprovingly at her. Didn't he realize his glare could even scare adults, Beth thought as Nancy seemed nervous and Rob's expression wasn't softening. "I wanted the best for my daughter and Charles wasn't. I knew they were in love, but instead of doing right by her, he did everything wrong. He impregnated her and failed to own up. I wasn't going to allow him to make my daughter and family a laughing stock so I gave Lisa an ultimatum. Either she got married to you or never would she step foot in my home ever again." She paused as she took a sip of water before she continued. "Lisa got married to you, as she worried over the baby more. She lost the child the next day after your wedding." Rob stared at his mother in law full of anguish in his eyes; thinking on how Lisa had silently moaned yet couldn't share her grief with him. Nancy had said that's how she acted during her monthlies. "Lisa fell pregnant three months later after the incidence and she did fall in love with you Rob but she feared if you knew the truth on how she tricked you into getting married, you would hate her. That was a secret she was meant to take to her grave. Charles would have ruined my daughter if I hadn't given her that ultimatum. For twenty three years my reputation has been spick and span but he was going to bring it all back."

Mr. Richards coughed and the wife attended to him as she gave him water to drink before settling down. "You see, I was born on the other side, were crime is rampant and people have loose morals. You know how hard it is to distance yourself from that life." Nancy stared at Rob who knew Charles history. Charles had managed to distance himself from his family as Robs father the senior Parker had helped him. Rob had always wished the best for his friend, that's why he had considered Beth as good for him. They would both have what they needed the most, a fresh start. He knew deep down Charles was a good man and Nancy was wrong to have separated Lisa from Charles. "Richard Reynolds was my fresh start." At that Beth gasped as Nancy chuckled and continued. "But my family bothered him so much, as he scraped one brother and sister from such and such a bind. Finally he became tired of me and my family. That's what would have happened to Lisa. Charles might be the odd one out in the family, but they would have found a way to take him back into the fold and Lisa would have been frustrated as her father was. He almost left me, you know that." She shook her head as she spoke, oblivious to the people listening to her. "For a one night stand, he wanted to give up everything. I found out she was just a mere sixteen year old, he had thought she was nineteen." She cackled with glee. "What a scandal it could have been. I handled it. I sent some people to teach her a lesson." It suddenly dawned on Beth why her mother suddenly changed as gran used to say and became a shadow of her former self. Someone scared her badly. "I made Rich promise he would never look for your mother nor get in contact with her, or I would reveal to the whole world he had raped a sixteen year old girl. That wasn't a relationship, a sixteen year old girl and he wanted to leave everything. Typical." She scoffed and continued, "He agreed to that but I didn't see what he had up his sleeve until after his death. He named his daughter Elizabeth Martins as owner of half of his assets, while the other was left to Lisa. They was the ranch, the townhouse and construction company. Half went to her." Everything fell into place at her last statement as Beth and Rob both realized why she looked like Lisa. They were sisters. Nancy chuckled, "I couldn't let that happen. Lose everything. She wasn't there when we built our life. Lisa, my beautiful daughter Lisa had somehow seen the will. She confronted me the day she died. Said Beth was her young sister and deserved to have something of her father since she never had anything. Ungrateful daughter she even had proof. She had done a DNA test." Beth thought back on the hug and her hair getting caught in Lisa's hair. "I tried to stop her, because she wanted to tell you. That's how she fell on the stairs." She sobbed but still continued, "I found out later she had been bluffing to catch me in a lie. I received the results a week later, at that time she was gone. Before she died, she entrusted Penny to you. She pleaded with me but I never honored her last wishes. Penny has always been yours Beth." Beth looked at the woman horrified as she wept and her husband stroked her hair. She moved towards her and hugged her. So many secrets and lies just to keep up a façade, she rather pitied her. They walked out of the yard in a daze. They were outside the car when Beth finally let up and wept and Rob engulfed her in his warm hug. She never got to see her father, he had died before she met him, and her other link Lisa was also gone. "Hush love," Rob comforted. He had misunderstood Lisa thinking she was selfish. She cared for her baby more and wanted to provide the best for him or her. Losing the baby might have crushed her, but she eventually rose above that. He remembered on the last day her saw her standing outside her mother's house and hollering, "I love you Pastor Robin Parker." She had looked so alive and beautiful. How had he forgotten that for a while? He wiped the tears off Beth before kissing her on the forehead. "Come on, let's go and get our children and go home." He advised and watched her smile as she thought of her little family and got into the car.

Epilogue

EVERYONE WAS IN A CELEBRATORY mood as they gathered around the table for a christmas dinner. Joan was giggling at Joey who Beth had pointed out wasn't a minister at all like her father but rather a lowly deacon, pulling Jos legs. She had merely rolled her eyes stating, "a good young man will do Beth." Aunt Courtney was there with her two girls, Hillary who was Beth's best friend and Heather her nemesis. How she had managed that, she wondered as Heather reminded her of how surlen Lisa used to be before she got to know her. Heather would come around one day. This had turned out to be a full house affair since her mother , aunt, Robs parents where also at the table hollering above the din like the rest not giving each other the opportunity to talk. She met her double or was it now her tripple, aunt Celestine and her three teenage daughters. They welcomed Beth into the fold and were also at the table hollering with the rest. Aunt Rose was already searching out for a husband for Abigail the first born who had turned eighteen a month ago and had inlisted Rob to do so. Beth sighed as she rather thought Tina and her mother were the best in the matchmaking business, since she was happy with their choice. She marveled at how things changed. From being just her and her mom, she had gained such a huge family. She stared at Nancy who sat right across from her feeding Penny some pureed peas and smiled. The woman was good to get along with and she didn't begrudge her. Beth had left everything in Nancy and Neils capable hands. She wasn't going to take away any of it, rather their children would benefit from the proceeds of the farm and company. Neil was on the side with tufts of hair shaped like horns very pronounced after Ryan had pulled at his head. Rob squeezed her hand from under the table and grinned. "so what do you think of our noisy family." She chuckled, "I love it. This is the best christmas gift ever."

"Really," he raised his brow at that since for a while he had been dazed when she told him she was expecting. Already they had two noisy children who never gave them the chance to get it on anymore. As if they had formed a pact of lets keep mommy and daddy from having an alone time. She had chuckled at his reaction and hugged him. "Thought you wanted a huge family since you are an only child," in which he had retorted, "That is your dream and not mine."

"Shall we," Rob asked as she nodded her head. The christmas festival took place on Christmas eve and had been a success. She could still hear the soft melodious voices of her small choir since they had recorded the whole thing and it was playing on the stereo. Though she doubted if the rest were even listening to it. She stood up with her husband as he cleared his throat and clinked on the glass with a fork. The family quietened down, including their two children. "Thank you all for joining us for the christmas dinner today." Rob went on to make a short speech before he settled down. Seeing his wife still standing and looking disapprovingly at him, he remembered the good news and stood up. "By the way, we have good news to share with you. We are pregnant." Ryan and Penny screamed as Rob stared at her and whispered, "told you." While the adults laughed and congradulated them. They plucked up their two children from their grandparents as they competed over who cried the most. "Merry Christmas to you all." They managed to shout before they left the room with their tearless, weepy kids.

The End

ALSO BY AUTHOR

A RISKY VENTURE

Yvette's childhood was one full of rejection and abandonment from people meant to love her until a kind old lady gave her a home. Now all grown up and successful she is skittish towards forming relationships especially with men. Jesse is disillusioned having had his heart broken by the woman he wanted to marry. As a joke to while away his time, he bets he could have Vee eating out of the palm of his hand in no time. Will he succeed in that. Make the stiff woman pliable or she will succeed in mending his broken heart?

THE INCONVENIENT MARRIAGE

Thia has always felt that Rod is her soul mate even though it has been years since they were together. A chance encounter at a high school reunion makes her see what's important except it might be too late and her husband Chad might divorce her on the spot when he discovers her betrayal.

Will she able to convince him that she truly is in love with him and not her ex. Chad is rather tired of being the second best in a relationship that should not have been formed in the first place. Will he manage to convince his wayward wife to see him and not another.

FINDING A HUSBAND FOR CISSY

Cissy's motto to her relationship troubles is to find another man who will cherish her. Except it's no longer relationships but marriages she is coming out and going into. She just can't stop from her retreat and wayward behavior. Is she destined to be one loathed by her children for not having any self-control or one man in her trend will finally succeed in making her remain married?

SWEET CRAZY LOVE

When Elsie Cooper wrote out her ten year plan, she never anticipated the detours she would have to make in fulfilling it. Not only did the pandemic that took the world by surprise make a dent over her wedding plans after school, she just had to fall in love with two men at the same time. One knew her dark past and accepted her, while another thought she was just a crazy twittering girl, and still young to be taken seriously. Find out what happens when Randy her supposedly uninterested friend finally sees her for the young beautiful mature woman that she is and Sean her longtime boyfriend proposes out of the blue before the set time therefore turning her well thought out plan askew again.

LOVING A COMPTON

Rita Duncan is horrified at finding out that she will be a mother before she is done with fulfilling her dream. What worsens the situation is the fact that the father of her unborn child is Sean Compton, her best friends' ex-fiancé. She can't remember their night together apart from the five hundred dollars; he considerately left on her bedside as proof of what he really thought about her. With her nicely planned out life, what is a girl to do apart from get rid of the problem and live happily ever after, except she is scared and she decides to look for help from her best friend who would definitely be pissed off once she finds out about her betrayal.

Nevertheless she is in desperate need of her help so she has clarity on what to do next.

Sean Compton is furious of having to chase after a woman who appears to employ every avoidance tactic she can think up. He wants to explain something to her but the ever evasive Rita will not let him. Finally he gives up and right on cue, the solution to his problem comes in the form of his ex-fiancée who drops a bombshell on him. Will he do the right thing or make the evasive Rita finally pay?

THE DESIGNER'S WICKED INTENTIONS

Aggy is torn between doing what society terms is right and following her heart. Tragedy strikes and that one chance she had before, fades away as her best friend changes to be what she has always wanted.

Indifferent.

Ethan has always loved Aggy yet she always found a reason for them not to be together. Finally he gives her what she longs for except she has changed her mind. So as to make sure it's not just a phase, he tests that resolve. Find out how they both finally get what they want.

THE PERFECT GENTLEMAN

Forced to leave the only home she knew, Sophia Daniels gives up her freedom and becomes Sparkle the number one gem of Madam's S establishment. She is hardened in everyway from being the naive girl she used to be. Life has been cruel and she only thinks of the present. Greg has been searching for his innocent Sophie who always saw the beauty of everything in the world. Out of frustration he agrees to an outrageous plan from his friend Dominic. Such is his shock when he discovers who Sparkle is. Will the ill-fated lovers finally be together or other forces want them to stay apart?

To find out more about my books and upcoming titles, you can go to the following sites:

https://www.facebook.com/vovosibbs/